SHINING IN THE DARK

Celebrating Twenty Years
of Lilja's Library

Edited by
Hans-Åke Lilja

G

GALLERY BOOKS
NEW YORK LONDON TORONTO SYDNEY NEW DELHI

———◆———

For all the readers of Lilja's Library.
If not for you, this book would never have happened!

For Stephen King. I'm up for 20 more years, I hope you are.

———◆———

TABLE OF CONTENTS

CELEBRATING TWENTY YEARS OF LILJA'S LIBRARY:
AN INTRODUCTION—*Hans-Åke Lilja* — 9

THE BLUE AIR COMPRESSOR:
A TELLING OF HORROR—*Stephen King* — 13

THE NET—*Jack Ketchum & P. D. Cacek* — 25

THE NOVEL OF THE HOLOCAUST—*Stewart O'Nan* — 53

AELIANA—*Bev Vincent* — 63

PIDGIN AND THERESA—*Clive Barker* — 77

AN END TO ALL THINGS—*Brian Keene* — 91

CEMETERY DANCE—*Richard Chizmar* — 101

DRAWN TO THE FLAME—*Kevin Quigley* — 107

THE COMPANION—*Ramsey Campbell* — 157

THE TELL-TALE HEART—*Edgar Allan Poe* — 171

A MOTHER'S LOVE—*Brian James Freeman* — 177

THE KEEPER'S COMPANION—*John Ajvide Lindqvist*
(translated from its original Swedish by Marlaine Delargy) — 183

CELEBRATING 20 YEARS OF LILJA'S LIBRARY:
AN AFTERWORD—*Hans-Åke Lilja* — 219

CELEBRATING TWENTY YEARS OF LILJA'S LIBRARY: AN INTRODUCTION

20 YEARS. TASTE it. 20 years! That is a very long time. What have you done in the last 20 years? I have gotten married. I've gotten two great kids. I've lived in three different houses. And most important (at least in the context of this book) I have run the site Lilja's Library—The World of Stephen King during all those 20 years. I haven't updated the site every day for those 20 years but I have done my very best to keep all my readers up to date on everything that has happened in Steve's Kingdom. And if I may say so myself (and since it's my book I may) I've done a pretty good job.

So, when the 20-year anniversary was just a year or so away I started thinking that I needed to celebrate it with something extra. I just couldn't let it pass unnoticed. At one point I spoke to Brian Freeman at Cemetery Dance about it and I think it was he who suggested that "Why don't we do an anthology to celebrate the site?". Well, why not I thought but if the idea would work I needed to get permission to use a story by Stephen King. I mean it would just not have worked to do a book to celebrate the 20-year anniversary of a site dedicated to Stephen King without including a story by the man himself, right? That would just be crazy.

So, I set out to get permission to use a story, and in mid-July I got the thumbs up to use "The Blue Air Compressor," a story that hasn't been published in any of Stephen King's collections. I guess you can imagine my excitement. If you can't, I can tell you that it included jumping, shouting and crazy laughter. With that story in place I could start to put the rest of the anthology together, which after getting the okay on "The Blue Air Compressor" seemed like the easy part to me. Boy was I wrong. Don't get me wrong, I loved every part of it but it was a totally new experience for me and I'm so glad I had Brian Freeman at my side to help me out. I had no clue about how the payment for something like this worked. I had no clue about writing contracts with authors.In fact, there was a lot I had no clue about but I got through it and as I said, I loved every aspect of it. I also got the chance to speak to some of the biggest authors out there. I actually spoke directly to most of the 13 (how fitting with 13 authors right?) authors that are in this anthology... and some that aren't. Some it took some time to get in touch with (it's not like if you could just Google them and get an email or phone number) and others responded in just a few hours after I had emailed them. Everyone that committed to joining me in the celebration either contributed a story they had published earlier or with an unpublished piece (it's a very exciting feeling to be one of the first to read a brand-new story). Six of the twelve stories (yes, one of the stories is a collaboration and therefore there are 13 authors and 12 stories) have not been published anywhere before this publication. Some of them were even written directly for this anthology. Of the six that have, many were only published in magazines. So, chances are that you'll read most of the stories in here for the first time. Something I'm very excited about.

An Introduction

One story was even originally written in my native language (Swedish) and that's "The Keeper's Companion" by John Ajvide Lindqvist. It was translated by Marlaine Delargy, and I was actually involved in some details with the translation with John, which was very exciting. I would never have imagined that I'd be consulted by the, in my opinion, biggest horror writer in Sweden.

The oldest story in this book is by Edgar Allan Poe. He wrote "The Tell Tale Heart" in 1843, more than 170 years ago and the newest story is "An End to All Things" by Brian Keene who finished it in mid-April of 2016. The anthology collects the horror and fear of 13 authors. Some I have just gotten to know, while I have known others for 20 years. Some are pure horror. Some will make you feel uncomfortable. Some will make you think. Some will make you cry and some will make you smile. My hope is that they will all entertain you and that you, like me, will love them all in their own way and once you finish the book...don't forget to say goodnight to your pets. You never know when you'll get another chance...

One last thing...

As I write this addition to my introduction in early April 2019, a little more than a year has passed since the first edition of Shining in the Dark was released. A book that was at first only meant to be released in the US has now been published in eight other countries (Bulgaria, Italy, Czech Republic, Germany, Sweden, UK, Serbia and Brazil) and is, as we speak, being considered by publishers in four more. Both Simon & Schuster Audio and Hodder & Stoughton have released it as an audio book, and now the time has come for Gallery Books to release it in trade paperback edition. Imagine if I had known back in 1998, when I asked Scribner for an Advance Readers Copy of Bag of Bones, that 21 years later they would be releasing a book I created. Mind-blowing!

THE BLUE AIR COMPRESSOR:
A TELLING OF HORROR

BY STEPHEN KING

THE HOUSE WAS tall, with an incredible slope-shingled roof. As he walked up toward it from the shore road, Gerald Nately thought it was almost a country in itself, geography in microcosm. The roof dipped and rose at varying angles above the main building and two strangely angled wings; a widow's walk skirted a mushroom-shaped cupola which looked toward the sea; the porch, facing the dunes and lusterless September scrub grass was longer than a Pullman car and screened in. The high slope of roof made the house seem to beetle its brows and loom above him. A Baptist grandfather of a house.

He went to the porch and, after a moment of hesitation, through the screen door to the fanlighted one beyond. There were only a wicker chair, a rusty porch swing, and an old discarded knitting basket to watch him go. Spiders had spun silk in the shadowy upper corners. He knocked.

There was silence, inhabited silence. He was about to knock again when a chair someplace inside wheezed deeply in its throat. It was a tired sound. Silence. Then the slow, dreadfully patient sound of old, overburdened feet finding their way up the hall. Counterpoint of cane: Whock... whock... whock...

The floorboards creaked and whined. A shadow, huge and unformed in the pearled glass, bloomed on the fanlight. Endless sound of fingers laboriously solving the riddle of chain, bolt, and hasp lock. The door opened. "Hello," the nasal voice said flatly. "You're Mr. Nately. You've rented the cottage. My husband's cottage."

"Yes." Gerald said, his tongue swelling in his throat. "That's right. And you're—"

"Mrs. Leighton," the nasal voice said, pleased with either his quickness or her name, though neither was remarkable. "I'm Mrs. Leighton."

this woman is so goddam fucking big and old she looks like oh jesus christ print dress she must be six-six and fat my god she's fat as a hog can't smell her white hair long white hair her legs those redwood trees ill that movie a tank she could be a tank she could kill me her voice is out of any context like a kazoo jesus if i laugh i can't laugh can she be seventy god how does she walk and the cane her hands are bigger than my feet like a goddam tank she could go through oak oak for christ's sake.

"You write." She hadn't offered him in.

"That's about the size of it," he said, and laughed to cover his own sudden shrinking from that metaphor.

"Will you show me some after you get settled?" she asked. Her eyes seemed perpetually luminous and wistful. They were not touched by the age that had run riot in the rest of her

wait get that written down
image: "age had run riot in her with luxuriant fleshiness:
she was like a wild sow let loose in a great and digni-
fied house to shit on the carpet, gore at the welsh dresser
and send the crystal goblets and wine-glasses all crash-
a-tumble, to trample the wine colored divans to lunatic
puffs of springs and stuffing, to spike the mirror-bright
finish of the great hall floor with barbarian hoof prints
and flying puddles of urine"
okay she's there it's a story i feel her

body, making it sag and billow.
"If you like," he said. "I didn't even see the cottage from the Shore Road, Mrs. Leighton. Could you tell me where—"

"Did you drive in?"

"Yes. I left my car over there." He pointed beyond the dunes, toward the road.

A smile, oddly one-dimensional, touched her lips. "That's why. You can only see a blink from the road; unless you're walking, you miss it." She pointed west at a slight angle away from the dunes and the house. "There. Right over that little hill."

"All right," he said, then stood there smiling. He really had no idea how to terminate the interview.

"Would you like to come in for some coffee? Or a Coca-Cola?"

"Yes," he said instantly.

She seemed a little taken back by his instant agreement. He had, after all, been her husband's friend, not her own. The face loomed above Gerald, moonlike, disconnected, undecided. Then she led him into the elderly, waiting house.

She had tea. He had Coke, Millions of eyes seemed to watch them. He felt like a burglar, stealing around the hidden fiction he could make of her, carrying only his own youthful winsomeness and a psychic flashlight.

My own name, of course, is Steve King, and you'll pardon my intrusion on your mind—or I hope you will. I could argue that the drawing aside of the curtain of presumption between reader and author is permissible because I am the writer: i.e., since it's my story I'll do any goddam thing I please with it—but since that leaves the reader out of it completely, that is not valid. Rule One for all writers is that the teller is not worth a tin tinker's fart when compared to the listener. Let us drop the matter, if we may. I am intruding for the same reason that the Pope defecates: we both have to.

You should know that Gerald Nately was never brought to the dock; his crime was not discovered. He paid all the same. After writing four twisted, monumental, misunderstood novels, he cut his own head off with an ivory-figured guillotine purchased in Kowloon.

I invented him first during a moment of eight o'clock boredom in a class taught by Carroll F. Terrell of the University of Maine English faculty. Dr. Terrell was speaking of Edgar A. Poe, and I thought

ivory guillotine Kowloon
twisted woman of shadows, like a pig
some big house
The blue air compressor did not come until later.

He did show her some of his writing. Not the important part, the story he was writing about her, but fragments of poetry, the spine of a novel that had ached in his mind for a year like embedded shrapnel, four essays. She was a perceptive critic, and addicted to marginal notations with her black felt-tip pen. Because she sometimes dropped in when he was gone to the village, he kept the story hidden in the back shed.

September melted into cool October, and the story was completed, mailed to a friend, returned with suggestions (bad ones), rewritten. He felt it was good, but not quite right. Some indefinable was missing. The focus was a shade fuzzy. He began to toy with the idea of giving it to her for criticism, rejected it, toyed with it again. After all, the story was her; he never doubted she could supply the final vector.

His attitude concerning her became increasingly unhealthy; he was fascinated by her huge, animalistic bulk, by the slow, tortoiselike way she trekked across the space between the house and the cottage,

image: "*mammoth shadow of decay swaying across shadowless sand, cane held in one twisted hand, feet clad in huge canvas shoes which pump and push at the coarse grains, face like a serving platter, puffy dough arms, breasts like drumlins, a geography in herself, a country of tissue*"

by her reedy, vapid voice; but at the same time he loathed her, could not stand her touch. He began to feel like the young man in "The Tell-Tale Heart," by Edgar A. Poe. He felt he could stand at her bedroom door for endless midnights, shining one ray of light on her sleeping eye, ready to pounce and rip the instant it flashed open.

The urge to show her the story itched at him maddeningly. He had decided, by the first day of December, that he would do it. The decision making did not relieve him, as it is supposed to do in the novels, but it did leave him with a feeling of antiseptic pleasure. It was right that it should be so—an omega that quite dovetailed with the alpha. And it was omega; he was vacating the cottage on the fifth of December. On this day he had just returned from the Stowe Travel Agency in Portland, where he had booked passage for the Far East. He had done this almost on the spur of the moment: the decision to go and the decision to show his manuscript to Mrs. Leighton had come together, almost as if he had been guided by an invisible hand.

In truth, he was guided; by an invisible hand—mine.

The day was white with overcast, and the promise of snow lurked in its throat. The dunes seemed to foreshadow the winter already, as Gerald crossed them between the slate-roofed house of her dominion and the low stone cottage of his. The sea, sullen and gray, curled on the shingle of beach. Gulls rode the swells like buoys.

He crossed the top of the last dune and knew she was there—her cane, with its white bicycle handgrip at the base, stood against the side of the door. Smoke rifted from the toy chimney.

Gerald went up the board steps, kicked sand from his high-topped shoes to make her aware of his presence, and then went in.

"Hi, Mrs. Leighton!"

But the tiny living room and the kitchen both stood empty. The ship's clock on the mantle ticked only for itself and for Gerald. Her gigantic fur coat lay draped over the rocker like some animal sail. A small fire had been laid in the fireplace, and it glowed and crackled busily. The tea pot was on the gas range in the kitchen, and one tea cup stood on the counter, still waiting for water. He peered into the narrow hall which led to the bedroom.

"Mrs. Leighton?"

Hall and bedroom both empty.

He was about to turn back to the kitchen when the mammoth chuckles began. They were large, helpless shakings of laughter, the kind that stays hidden for years and ages like wine. (There is also an Edgar A. Poe story about wine.)

The chuckles evolved into large bellows of laughter. They came from behind the door to the right of Gerald's bed, the last door in the cottage. From the toolshed.

my balls are crawling like in grammar school the old bitch she's laughing she found it the old fat shebitch goddam her goddam her goddam her you old whore you're doing that 'cause i'm out here you old shebitch whore you piece of shit

He went to the door in one step and pulled it open. She was sitting next to the small space heater in the shed, her dress pulled up over oak-stump knees to allow her to sit cross-legged, and his manuscript was held, dwarfed, in her bloated hands.

Her laughter roared and racketed around him. Gerald Nately saw bursting colors in front of his eyes. She was a slug, a maggot, a gigantic crawling thing evolved in the cellar of the shadowy house by the sea, a dark bug that had swaddled itself in grotesque human form.

In the flat light from the one cobwebbed window her face became a hanging graveyard moon, pocked by the sterile craters of her eyes and the ragged earthquake rift of her mouth.

"Don't you laugh," Gerald said stiffly.

"Oh Gerald," she said, laughing all the same. "This is such a bad story. I don't blame you for using a penname. it's—" she wiped tears of laughter from her eyes. "It's abominable!"

He began to walk toward her stiffly.

"You haven't made me big enough, Gerald. That's the trouble. I'm too big for you. Perhaps Poe, or Dostoyevsky, or Melville... but not you, Gerald. Not you. Not you."

She began to laugh again, huge racking explosions of sound.

"Don't you laugh," Gerald said stiffly.

The toolshed, after the manner of Zola:

Wooden walls, which showed occasional chinks of light, surrounded rabbit traps hung and slung in corners; a pair of dusty, unstrung snow-shoes; a rusty space heater showing flickers of yellow flame like cat's eyes; rakes; a shovel; hedge clippers; an ancient green hose coiled like a garter snake; four bald tires stacked like doughnuts; a rusty Winchester rifle with no bolt; a two-handed saw; a dusty workbench covered with nails, screws, bolts, washers, two hammers, a plane, a broken level, a dismantled carburetor which once sat inside a 1949 Packard convertible; a 4 hp. air-compressor painted electric blue, plugged into an extension cord running back into the house.

"Don't you laugh," Gerald said again, but she continued to rock back and forth, holding her stomach and flapping the manuscript with her wheezing breath like a white bird.

His hand found the rusty Winchester rifle and he pole-axed her with it.

Most horror stories are sexual in nature.

I'm sorry to break in with this information, but feel I must in order to make the way clear for the grisly conclusion of this piece, which is (at least psychologically) a clear metaphor for fears of sexual impotence on my part. Mrs. Leighton's large mouth is symbolic of the vagina; the hose of the compressor is a penis. Her female bulk huge and overpowering, is a mythic representation of the sexual fear that lives in every male, to a greater or lesser degree: that the woman, with her opening, is a devourer.

In the works of Edgar A. Poe, Stephen King, Gerald Nately, and others who practice this particular literary form, we are apt to find locked rooms, dungeons, empty mansions (all symbols of the womb); scenes of living burial (sexual impotence); the dead returned from the grave (necrophilia); grotesque monsters or human beings (externalized fear of the sexual act itself); torture and/or murder (a viable alternative to the sexual act).

These possibilities are not always valid, but the post-Freud reader and writer must take them into consideration when attempting the genre.

Abnormal psychology has become a part of the human experience.

She made thick, unconscious noises in her throat as he whirled around madly, looking for an instrument; her head lolled brokenly on the thick stalk of her neck.

He seized the hose of the air-compressor.

"All right," he said thickly. "All right, now. All right."

bitch fat old bitch you've had yours not big enough is that right well you'll be bigger you'll be bigger still

He ripped her head back by the hair and rammed the hose into her mouth, into her gullet. She screamed around it, a sound like a cat.

Part of the inspiration for this story came from an old E.C. horror comic book, which I bought in a Lisbon Falls drugstore. In one particular story, a husband and wife murdered each other simultaneously in mutually ironic (and brilliant) fashion. He was very fat; she was very thin. He shoved the hose of an air compressor down her throat and blew her up to dirigible size. On his way downstairs a booby-trap she had rigged fell on him and squashed him to a shadow.

Any author who tells you he has never plagiarized is a liar. A good author begins with bad ideas and improbabilities and fashions them into comments on the human condition.

In a horror story, it is imperative that the grotesque be elevated to the status of the abnormal.

The compressor turned on with a whoosh and a chug. The hose flew out of Mrs. Leighton's mouth. Giggling and gibbering, Gerald stuffed it back in. Her feet drummed and thumped on the floor. The flesh of her cheeks and diaphragm began to swell rhythmically. Her eyes bulged, and became glass marbles. Her torso began to expand.

here it is here it is you lousy louse are you big enough yet are you big enough

The compressor wheezed and racketed. Mrs. Leighton swelled like a beach ball. Her lungs became straining blowfish.

Fiends! Devils! Dissemble no more! Here! Here! It is the beating of his hideous heart!

She seemed to explode all at once.

Sitting in a boiling hotel room in Bombay, Gerald rewrote the story he had begun at the cottage on the other side of the world. The original title had been "The Hog." After some deliberation he retitled it "The Blue Air Compressor."

He had resolved it to his own satisfaction. There was a certain lack of motivation concerning the final scene where the fat old woman was murdered, but he did not see that as a fault. In "The Tell-Tale Heart," Edgar A. Poe's finest story, there is no real motivation for the murder of the old man, and that was as it should be. The motive is not the point.

She got very big just before the end; even her legs swelled up to twice their normal size. At the very end, her tongue popped out of her mouth like a party-favor.

After leaving Bombay, Gerald Nately went on to Hong Kong, then to Kowloon. The ivory guillotine caught his fancy immediately.

As the author, I can see only one correct omega to this story, and that is to tell you how Gerald Nately got rid of the body. He tore up the floor boards of the shed, dismembered Mrs. Leighton, and buried the sections in the sand beneath.

When he notified the police that she had been missing for a week, the local constable and a State Policeman came at once. Gerald entertained them quite naturally, even offering them coffee. He heard no beating heart, but then, the interview was conducted in the big house.

On the following day he flew away, toward Bombay, Hong Kong, and Kowloon.

THE NET

BY *JACK KETCHUM & P.D. CACEK*

5/6/2003 11:22 PM

ANDREW—

I can't BELIEVE you picked me over all the other women in that chatroom!

5/6/2003 11:31 PM

CASSANDRA—

Are you kidding? I liked a lot of the others well enough—Mugu, Wicked. But some of them...jeez...when the hell is Maya gonna get off her high horse? Or Babycrazed for that matter. And tell me, please, when is Flit gonna develop a brain?

But I'd think my reasons for wanting to write just to you ought to be pretty obvious. You're smart, you're funny, and from the way you wrote about little kids the other day I know you're caring too. Do you have kids, by the way? Odd thing about chat rooms. You can be on for weeks and never really get to know the people you're talking to. Anyhow, glad you accepted my invitation. Look forward to hearing from you.

Best,

Andrew

5/7/2003 10:01 PM
ANDREW—

No, I don't have any kids of my own... but I'd love to. One day. Right now I have to be satisfied with spoiling my niece and nephew. They're just babies, only two and four, but I figure if their only aunt can't spoil them, who can?

And you're right ... sometimes you can chat to someone for months and never really get a clear idea of who—or what—they are. It's funny, though, because I feel I know more about you than I do some of the people I've known for years. For instance—that time you and Tigerman got "into it" about experimenting on animals and how mad he got because you said animals have just as much right to live without fear and pain as people do ... and he told you to go "F" yourself. You could have said that, too, but you didn't. You stayed a gentleman to the end and that's what I suspect you are, Andrew ... a gentle man. Hope to hear from you soon. Bye—

Cassandra

P.S.: Call me Cassie ... all my real friends do. :-)

P.P.S: What kind of music do you like? I just love the stuff from 80's! 'Bye again

5/7/2003 11:00 PM
CASSIE—

Tigerman's a jerk. I didn't want to say that with everybody else listening in but since it's just you and me now I feel freer. I never liked the guy much, tell the truth. He always seemed...I dunno...either to be hiding something or hiding behind something. Getting "into it" with me was about as open as he got. So maybe I accomplished something :-) Who knows?

Are you planning on going back there again? To Singlechat I mean. Don't really think I want to. I guess I'd just like to stay with talking to you for a while if you don't mind.

Music? All kinds. No headbanger or rap though. 50's stuff, Beatles-era, country—I even listen to opera and show tunes now and then. THERE, I'VE SAID IT! SHOW TUNES! Hope it doesn't cost me our relationship:-) But my favorite's definitely the blues. I can listen to the blues all night long. It's good no matter how you're feeling—happy, sad, whatever. It seems to touch something in me. Always has.

Gotta go. Need to go change the litterbox. My desk and computer are in a little alcove right off the bathroom. It's a kind of dressing-room I adapted into a study. But when Cujo's just used the litter it can get pretty stinky. One of the problems living in New York is that you can't let 'em go outside. They'd be meat in minutes. Don't suppose you're a cat-lover, are you?

Stay in touch, okay?

Andrew

P.S.: Thanks for calling me a gentleman. And a gentle man. I try to be.

Best,

Andrew

5/7/2003 11:20 PM

ANDREW—

I know what you mean about Tigerman. It did seem like he was hiding something—the way he got so angry when anybody challenged him. He really was beginning to creep me out. I felt the same way when Maya started talking about...you know... about how she thought it was okay to have as many boyfriends as she wanted just so long as they didn't know each other. I don't think it's okay and I wanted to tell her so—but I didn't feel I could. Like you said, not with everybody listening. Guess I'm just old fashioned in some ways...which is why I don't think

I'll ever go back to Singlechat. Besides, I don't have to now. I'd much rather "chat" with you :-)

I LOVE show tunes, too, so our relationship's fine. <blush> And I really like the Blues—especially on rainy nights. I like to turn the music way down, so the rain against the window sounds like it's part of the song and just lay in bed and listen. Sometimes I even fall asleep listening, it's so beautiful.

OHMYGOD...I LOVE cats and Cujo's a great name! (Please tell me Cujo's not as big as that dog in Stephen King's book! If he/she is you'd better go change that litter box QUICK! Eek!) I've had cats all my life...but not right now. I lost my cat, Sgt. Stripes, last Halloween. He was fifteen when he died and I'd had him since he was seven weeks old. It was hard...still is hard to think about him without wanting to cry. He was a BIG guy—twenty-eight pounds before he got sick—an orange tabby with gold eyes. I think he thought he was a dog because he used to follow me around the house and "wag" his tail...and sleep with me at night. It was nice, you know, feeling him next to me. That's the hardest part...being alone at night. I miss him so much.

Wow—got a little blue there. Sorry.

You live in New York City. That is so cool! We're practically neighbors! I live in Pennsylvania, a little town called Warminster—which I think is Lenni Lenape (Native American) for "Wide Spot in Road. Don't Blink."

Gotta go, too. Have a ton of paperwork to do. Give Cujo a hug for me.

—Cassie

5/8/2003 9:22 PM

CASSIE—

Fact is, Cujo was the runt of her litter. She's about half the size of most cats. And guess what? She's an orange tabby just like Sgt. Stripes—though her eyes are green. How about that? Something else we have in common!

It's okay to get blue sometimes. I sure do.

It's okay to be old-fashioned too, especially when it comes to relationships. Last relationship I had lasted a year, the one before that two years, and the one before that three years. Oooops—I guess they're getting shorter and shorter! But I've always been a one-woman guy. Even here in New York, where I guess there are plenty of opportunities, I've never dated more than one woman at a time. Don't believe in it.

Warminster, Pennsylvania. I looked it up on the map. Damn! that really isn't very far. What is it, about two-and-a-half, three hours from NY? Funny. On the Net you never know where people are writing from unless for some reason they tell you. You could have lived in L.A. or Michigan or Alaska for godsakes! Neighbors! Cool!

If this is too forward, let me know. No problem. But I'm wondering what you look like. I'd tell you what I look like but you called me a gentleman, right? And a gentleman always figures, ladies first.

All best,
Andrew

5/8/2003 11:32 PM

DEAR ANDREW, (HOPE you don't mind the "dear"...but that's part of being "old fashioned" too...)

And I'm glad you're old-fashioned. I sort of knew you would be. I'm sorry your last relationship ended so soon after it started but that just means it wasn't the right one. I know about that too. My last "serious" one lasted almost two years and...well, let's just say it didn't end on a very happy note. He wanted something I wasn't prepared to give...

I don't date a lot. Never really saw much use in just "going out" with someone. Maybe that's because I hadn't found a gentleman yet. Till now, that is...

Ooops. That was a little forward, wasn't it? <BLUSH!>

Okay, you asked me what I looked like...well, first clue—Cujo and I have something in common. No, I don't have orange stripes! My eyes are green...but that's all I'm going to say for now...:-)

I don't know what it's like where you are but Spring doesn't seem to know what it wants this year. 70s one day and 50s the next and RAIN, humidity. Humidity makes my hair go all curly. Ooops! now you know I have hair! Okay, it's dark brown hair in fact with red highlights. It used to be very long, down to my waist when I was little, but that would take FOREVER to dry. Hope you're not disappointed but my hair's short now, curly in summer and kind of "shaggy" the rest of the time.

Okay, I'm sort of tall...all legs, was what my father used to say. Still does when he wants to get me to blush. Which isn't hard to do. <blush>

Can I tell you something? I've always thought a man is as handsome as he acts, what he does and how he behaves. Looks aren't as important to me as what's inside. But...it's YOUR turn now. Tell me what Andrew looks like. If you want, that is. Gotta go now...more later...promise.

OO (hugs)

Cassie

P.S.: New York's only an hour and forty-five minutes away. I checked Map-Quest. :-)

5/9/2003 1:03 AM
DEAR CASSIE,

I used to have long hair too—way back in the hippie days—and cut it for the same reason. Pain in the butt to dry...I'm 5'10", about 140 pounds, dark hair, in pretty good shape for a guy my age. My eyes change slightly depending on what I'm wearing. My driver's license says "blue" but they range from blue to gray to amber.

You're only an hour and forty-five minutes away? Guess I didn't read that map too well.

Tell me more. Are your mom and dad alive? Mine are both gone, my mother for many years now, my father for seven. I think I mentioned back in Singlechat that I'm an only child. You said you have a sister. Any other siblings? Just curious. Family seems to get more important to me as I grow older—or in my case, the lack of one. Don't mean to sound sorry for myself—it's just a fact I deal with. I've got some aunts and uncles and cousins but I'm not really close to them. Probably that's why I like cats so much—surrogate family. :-)

Write soon, okay?

XOXOXOX Andrew

5/9/2003 6:34 PM

DEAR ANDREW,

Your eyes sound remarkable—magical in fact. Makes me wish my eyes were something other than plain old green. I'd say jade green, but I wouldn't want to lie to you. :-)

There is one thing...I hate talking about myself, as I'm sure you noticed in Singlechat, I'm basically shy and pretty uninteresting when you come right down to it...but...okay—my friends say I look "hot" in a bathing suit. <BLUSH!!!!!!!!!>

Anyhow, you wanted to know about my parents (still blushing, by the way.) They're both alive and quite active. My Mother was a "Stay-at-Home-Mom" when my sister and I were little, but has recently gone back to school! She wants to get her Teaching Credential and my dad and I think it's great. My Dad, by the way, owns his own Travel Agency—we've had a LOT of great vacations! In fact, my Mom and Dad will be going on a "Second Honeymoon" in a few days—to Hawaii for a week. Don't know what I'll do with myself while they're gone—since I live with them (saves on rent)—but I'm sure I'll think of something.

I understand about feeling distant from family. My sister and I are a bit distant. I'd never tell her this but I think she tends to put her career (Real Estate) before her children, while

I think being a mom is the best "job" a woman can have. On the other hand, her being so into work lets me spend a lot more time with Mandy and Jamie (my niece and nephew) so I guess there's an upside to everything. Like tonight...which is why this e-mail's so short—my sister's asked me to baby-sit and I plan to spoil those kids ROTTEN! I've rented MONSTERS, INC, SHREK, and MY favorites, ARISTOCATS and GAY PURR-EE!

Probably sounds like a really boring night...right? So what are YOUR favorite movies? Color? Books? Inquiring minds want to know. Hugs to your kitty....and you.

x
Cassie

5/9/2003 7:10 PM
DEAR CASSIE,

Your movie-night doesn't sound boring at all. I think it's great you're into kids. Favorite movies, books? That's hard. Color is easy. Black. But the reason the other two are hard is that although what I do for a living is write freelance ad copy, my goal's to become a real writer. Fiction. Been trying for about five years now, ever since I quit my nine-to-five at the agency. So far, lots of rejection letters but not much else, though some of them have been very encouraging. Point is, because of that I read constantly, and I see movies all the time. Need to see what's out there. So to pick favorites is almost impossible. The book I'm reading right now is great—Dennis Lehane's SHUTTER ISLAND, about two detectives investigating an escape from a mental institution. I rented REMAINS OF THE DAY again the night before last. Love that movie. So lonely, so sad. But the list would have to go on and on....

You live with your parents, huh? God! you must have a hell of a good relationship! I remember I couldn't WAIT to get out of there, on my own, as soon as possible. I know that rents being what they are these days a lot of younger folks are doing that but there's no way I could have. How old are you, anyway? If you don't mind my asking. I'm going to risk something now and tell you that I'll be forty-six in November—I suspect that's more than a few years older than you. And I hope it doesn't change things between us. Say it ain't so! :-)

And as long as I'm in a risky mood tonight I'll admit to one other thing. We're completely on the same page, you and I, about what the important things are between people. But long legs, green eyes, brown-red hair and "hot in a bathing suit...." I'm getting a mental picture of you. And I gotta admit that I like what I see. :-)

XOXOXOXOX Andrew

5/10/2003 1:05 AM
DEAR ANDREW...

Sorry it took me so long to get back to you but the evening was a DISASTER! My loving sister didn't tell me that Jamie was sick—let's just say "leaking" at both ends, poor baby. I had to make sure Mandy didn't get too close and that was hard because she loves her big brother SO much. So she started crying and Jamie started crying and...needless to say they weren't very interested in watching movies. :-(I'm exhausted, but couldn't collapse until I answered you. See how important you are? <g>

Black's another thing we have in common! I love it and always try to wear something black every day (sometimes you can't see it, but it's there.) And OMYGOD! you're a writer! I've never known a real writer. That is so...awesome (as the kids say.) I hope this isn't pushy or anything but could you send me a story? I'd love to read one. Honest. I really do need something to read anyway. Just finished a book you'd probably love—A DANCE FOR EMILIA by Peter S. Beagle. It's about a man who comes back from the dead in his cat. It's beautiful and made me cry at the end. What can I say, I'm a big softie. I love stories that have a bittersweet ending. I did see REMAINS OF THE DAY. And cried.

Then I saw Anthony Hopkins in SILENCE OF THE LAMBS. EEEEEEEEK!

But, Sir (spoken with a heavy Southern Belle accent beneath a fluttering fan,) y'all should know better'n to ask a lady her age. (Flutter, flutter.) Let's just say—ah'm—old enough.

Can you really SEE me? It's funny but I think you can. You can see the REAL me and that makes me feel very...special. See me right now as I write this, in bed, on my laptop...in my very short, very RED nightgown.

Can you see that?

Goodnight and XOXOXOXOXOX back.

Luv,

Cassie

5/10/2003 1:25 AM

DEAR CASSIE,

"Very short, very red nightgown...?" Phew! And you expect me to SLEEP now? <g>

I'll get a copy of the Beagle book. Sounds good. And I'll be glad to send you a story, too. I know just the one. It's called RETURNS, and it's also about a cat...and believe it or not, a ghost! The coincidences just keep piling up here. It really is wonderful. Thank god we got out of that damn chat room and into this.

Sometimes late-night e-mails seem almost like distress calls to me, you know? Like some sad lonely S.O.S. tapped out into cyberspace. But yours aren't like that at all. They make my day, Cassie. They really do.

Luv back atcha, and

XOXOXOXOXOXOXOXOXOXOXOXOXOXOXOXOX

Andrew

P.S.: Whoops, forgot. I don't know your address. I guess I got a little bit carried away back there...

Andrew

5/10/2003 8:15 AM

:-) I don't think you got carried away at all. I think you're pretty wonderful. I know we haven't known each other for very long—on or off the chat-room—but I already feel a connection with you that I've never really had with anyone else. Does that sound really weird to you? Hope not, because I wanted to be honest with you about this.

My address. 119 North Street Road, Warminster, Pa. 18974. But you could send the story as an attachment...so I could read it sooner. Hint, hint, HINT. Now I HAVE to get going or I'll be LATE!

XoXoXoXoXoXo

Cassie

5/10/2003 2:01 PM

DEAR CASSIE,

Okay...gulp...the story's attached. I can only hope you're kinder to it than some editors have been.

Early riser, huh? Me, I'm a night person. Don't even want to TALK to anybody before ten in the morning...

It occurs to me now that it's awfully good of you to trust me with your street address after only knowing me from Singlechat and these e-mails. A lot of women wouldn't. I guess I must be doing something right :-) And you...well, you tell me I'm wonderful and I'm kinda floored by that, it's been a long time since anybody's called me that, and I just want to say...hell, I dunno what I want to say...only that (and don't get scared now, okay?) I may be falling for you just a little. Just a little. Is it okay to say that? Jeez—I better sign off now before I put my entire LEG into my mouth, not just my foot.

Love,

Andrew

5/10/2003 4:00 PM

DEAREST ANDREW,

Haven't even opened your story but I had to send this first—it's more than OKAY because I think I'm...falling for you too. And I do trust you. More than I've trusted anyone for a very long time.

Okay. Just HAD to say that. Now...on to your story. I'll write as soon as I read it. Promise, promise, promise.

<kiss>

Cassie

5/10/2003 5:15 PM

DEAREST ANDREW—

Oh. My. God.

Your story is...beyond beautiful. Those editors must be crazy. I started crying after I read it the first time and I'm still crying. But don't get me wrong...I'm crying because it's so BEAUTIFUL. You're brilliant! At first I thought the man came back as a ghost for his girlfriend, and then, when I realized it was for his cat...Andrew, that was so touching. And then when the girlfriend has the guy from the pound come over to have the cat destroyed...

Wait a minute. I'm crying again. Gotta get more Kleenex.

Okay, I'm back.

But that part...I wanted the ghost to hit her, beat her up, do SOMETHING to stop her. Then I realized it was okay, that he was there to see his cat through. Andrew, you touched my heart and let me finally get all the grief for Stripes out in a good way. Thank you so very much. I loved the story, Andrew. Really. And I love you for sharing it with me.

What else is there to say?

XOXOXOXOXOX Cassie

5/10/2003 7:33 PM
MY GOD, CASSIE...

You can't begin to know how much this means to me. You really can't. I was cooking dinner, something reheatable that would last me for a few days. Just something simple, y'know? Chicken tarragon in a garlic/wine sauce. Anyhow I was letting it simmer a while before I started on the rice and asparagus and I thought, check your e-mail, maybe she's read the attachment by now. And I'm amazed by your response. Not so much to the writing, though nobody's ever exactly called me brilliant before, but your response to the heart of the story, that I touched you so deeply, that you felt the story had even helped you heal a bit. That's so fulfilling, so important and beautiful to hear.

And Cassie? You know what? You just said you loved me...

I know you mean you loved me because of the story. I understand that. But do you think it's possible for two people to fall in love—REALLY in love—just by writing back and forth like this? Never having met? Never having touched or kissed? Never having even used the phone for godsakes? It feels so strange to me but know what? it feels good. Better than I've felt in years.

Uh-oh. Cujo's throwing up again. Only thing wrong with cats are furballs. Though she's been doing it a lot lately, dammit. I better go attend to it. But furball or no furball, I'm smiling now. Can you see it? Big wide grin.

Love you, Cassie,
Andrew

5/10/2003 9:58 PM
DEAREST ANDREW,

It wasn't just the story. And I do believe that people can fall in love without ever having touched or seen each other. I think we're proof. I love you, Andrew. Not your words. Not your talent. Not your brilliance. You. The real you. Your heart.

Plus hey, you can cook! My mother says I'd better find a man who can cook because I can barely boil water. One thing we DON'T have in common is garlic, though. I'm allergic. Does that make you think less of me? :-)

Poor Cujo. Hope her tummy feels better soon. Send her my love...as I send it to you.

All my love,

Cassie

5/12/2003 3:34 AM

Oh Cassie, I wish I could tell you how much I care, how much your last e-mail makes me feel. But right now I think something awful's happened—or something awful's about to happen. I don't want to go into it right away and alarm you because maybe that would turn out to be unnecessary and everything will be fine. But I gotta sign off right now. I'll write when I can.

I love you too, Cassie! I love you too! A

5/12/2003 8:05 AM

DEAR ANDREW,

What's wrong? Tell me. Please. I love you, and that's all that matters.

Love,

Cassie

5/12/2003 11:25 PM

Andrew? What's going on? Please write. PLEASE....

Love, Cassie

5/13/2003 8:10 AM

Andrew—what's happened? Can't you tell me? Is it something I said? Please let me know. Whatever it is, we can work it out. I know we can.

I REALLY love you—Cassie

5/15/2003 12:45 AM
   Andrew? What did I DO?

5/15/2003 9:55 PM
   Oh jesus, Cassie, honey, I'm so sorry to have put you through this. I can't believe I was so thoughtless. I haven't even looked at the computer. Couldn't bring myself to. I should have written so much sooner. I'd better explain.

   Friday afternoon I was working on some ad copy and I heard Cujo coughing in the kitchen. She didn't sound like she does when she's throwing a fur ball. It was this hacking cough. I went in and there she was on the floor, this cough hacking away at her from deep within. I almost thought she was choking. I got her some olive oil, which she'll take when it IS a fur ball but she wouldn't have anything to do with it.

   Finally it subsided and she retreated to the hall closet—there's a box of books there where she likes to sleep sometimes. I went back to work, worried but thinking maybe it was just some passing cat-thing. Then at dinnertime she wouldn't eat. I figured it was probably a bug or something but I kept an eye on her anyway. She seemed peaceful enough. Purred when I petted her. She wouldn't come out of the closet though. And then that night, about two in the morning, she woke me up coughing again, worse this time, hunched on her box and her eyes were tearing and it was like she couldn't get her breath, you know? so I wet a dish towel under warm water and wiped her eyes and mouth and nose and saw she was frothing at the mouth. And that scared the hell out of me. So I got her in her cat box and got a cab to the vet's. They have an emergency service all night long.

   The vet was somebody I'd never seen before and she was awfully young but she was very kind. She could see I was a mess. She diagnosed acute respiratory distress and gave her a shot of Cortizone to ease her breathing and it did help, I could see pretty much right away. I waited while they took her upstairs

for an x-ray and a while later Dr. Morris—that was her name—
came down and showed it to me on the light-board. Her lungs
were completely flecked with what looked like motes of dust,
but were really droplets of moisture. They looked like photos
you see of the milky way there were so many. They were THAT
DENSE, Cassie. And now I was really afraid for her.

Dr. Morris said she wanted to drain the lungs immediately
and start her on a heavy dose of antibiotics, that they wanted to
keep her overnight for observation. If worse came to worst, they
could knock her out and intubate her until hopefully the antibiotics took hold. I said whatever it takes. She said it was going
to be expensive and I said I don't care about the money, never
mind the money, whatever it takes. By then I was practically
crying. She told me to go home and get some sleep, that they'd
call me if there was any change. I went home and wrote to you.
That last e-mail. I drank a glass full of straight scotch and it did
was it was supposed to do, knocked me out, and I went to sleep.

They called at quarter to five in the morning. Almost dawn.
Said Cujo was failing fast and what did I want to do? I said just
hold her for me if you can, I'll be right there. I got there just in
time to feel her breathing stop, her heart stop, her eyes wide
open looking straight into mine as though she could see me.
I buried my face in her neck and cried and cried.

I'm crying now.

You see why I couldn't write, Cassie? I wish I could call you.
Can I call you? I need to talk to somebody now or I'll go crazy
and the only creature on earth other than you I could talk to is
gone now.

Love,

Andrew

5/15/2003 9:25 PM

Oh God, Andrew...just got your message. I'm crying too.
Can't talk right now. Can't write anymore. Give me a minute—I'll write back. I promise. I promi

5/15/2003 11:20 PM

My love.

I said I'd write back in a moment—and here it is, almost two hours later. I'm so sorry for not being able to get back to you sooner but...your loss, your horrible loss brought all the memories of Stripes back and I lost it, too. God that sounds so selfish...I hate myself for that, for failing you like that. But please, don't hate me—I couldn't stand it. I'm back and I'm here for you now. If you still want me to be...

Andrew, my darling Andrew I'm so sorry about Cujo. All I can say is how sorry I am and that I wish I could hold you and comfort you right now...I want to hold you, Andrew, so you'll feel safe to cry out all the sadness you feel. No one held me when Stripes died. I hid in my room...like now...and cried silently... like now.

But I AM holding you, Andrew—can you feel my arms around you? I hope you can, I really do. Because I love you and want to help you through. And I wish I could call...but my stupid father is still on the phone...making stupid last-minute "vacation arrangements" that HAVE to be done RIGHT THIS MINUTE! God! I wish I had my own place because if I did I'd be on the phone, talking to you...and telling you to come here, to come to me, to be with me so I can share what you feel.

And maybe you can. My parents leave tomorrow, Andrew... and maybe by morning you'll feel a little better—not a lot, I know, but a little maybe. If you do, why don't you think about coming down? You said you needed me. But I need you, too, Andrew. I need to help you through this because I LOVE YOU. I love you, Andrew. And I wish I could hold you right now.

What else can I do?

Love always,

Cassie

P.S.: You called me honey.

5/15/2003 11:25 PM
CASSIE—

When do they leave? I'm THERE. God, yes!
XOXOXOXOXOX A.

5/15/2003 11:28 PM
MY LOVE,

They leave tomorrow afternoon. I'll be here, alone. Whole house to myself. Please come...please.

XOXOXOXOXOXOXOXOXOXOXOXOXOXOXOXOXOXO-
XOXOXOXOXOXOXOXOXO

All my love,
Cassie

FROM THE JOURNAL OF ANDREW SKY:

I wish she'd sent me her phone number. Wonder why she didn't? It could be she's afraid of just this—that I might be tempted to chicken out at the last minute. Which I am. Maybe she anticipated that.

There's a real temptation not to show.

If I want to be there by nightfall I've got to leave in about an hour. No later. I've been procrastinating on leaving all day, ever since this morning staring into the mirror doing what I do every morning, shaving, brushing my teeth, looking at the same face I see every day. For the first time it struck me as a hard face, too few smile-lines and too many traces of frowns.

What can she possibly see in me?

I woke up all excited and an hour later I was depressed and worried and I've stayed that way all afternoon. I went out shopping at the Food Emporium. I corrected the Iona College ad copy that's due in the mail on Tuesday. I answered some e-mail—hoping, I think, that there'd be one from Cassie saying please don't come, this is a mistake, I'm not ready. There wasn't any.

It's me who's not ready.

I haven't even met her yet and I feel like I've lost her already.

What a fucking mess I am, huh?

I think of Laura and all I'd hoped for with her and I still get a knot in my gut, I still want to smash something. Hell, back then I did smash a few things—half the dishes in the sink, the lamp beside the bed—and all it got me were credit card bills for replacing them. What I needed to replace was Laura. But there was no replacing Laura. No way.

I couldn't replace the feeling of her beside me asleep in my bed or how cool I felt walking down the street with my arm around her waist, my woman, this woman more beautiful and successful than I'd ever thought could possibly be attracted to a guy like me but who said that she was mine and I was hers now, made me promise to always be hers no matter what. I remember laughing and saying who else's could I be?

And it was true. Who else's?

Nobody's. Before or since.

Not a single human being even touched me after Laura. Not until Cassie.

I don't even know for sure why I surfed my way into that dumb chatroom.

I think I was looking for a porn chat, really. Or maybe I was warming up to that. I looked at a lot of porn for a while. Another dumb escape. So it could very well be that I was building up the courage for a little porno-chat that day. Something at least remotely exciting. Maybe I'll flip back through these pages at some point and see if I entered it here.

Not that it matters.

But for over a year I'd felt as hard as my goddamn wall. Harder. It was a way to get by I guess. Tough it out. What few friends I had left that goddamn Laura didn't take along with her I put off and continue to put off and make excuses for not seeing because I know damn well I've become a bore on the subject as on most subjects like the goddamn copy I write for a living and the goddamn city I live in that won't even let you smoke in a bar anymore. And I will not be a bore. I have some pride.

I talked to my cat instead. You couldn't bore Cujo.

But if this building weren't pretty well soundproofed the neighbors might have had me locked up. I ranted and raved. I cried. I was howling at the moon here.

Cujo didn't mind.

Cujo was unshakable.

She could cure any hurt with that purr of hers. At least for a little while, until the hurt came back again.

But without her now this being alone just kills me. I'm in a city of how many million people? and I've never felt so completely cut off and alone. I might as well be some loony old hermit off in the Maine woods somewhere.

And whose fault is that? Mine of course.

Laura didn't leave for no reason. She left me for the same reason I'm pretty much unemployable—except as what I am, a free-lancer.

I never had a boss in my entire life who I didn't go off on at one time or another. I've lost more jobs than my TV has cable stations. I have this problem with author-ity figures I guess, with anybody who has power over me. Back when I could afford a shrink instead of just this journal Marty and I talked about it a lot. Goes all the way back to my parents we decided. A hell of lot of good that did me.

But Laura had power over me. The kind of power only a woman you love can have. More than I should have let her have. I realize that now. And I had this temper. We fought like cats and dogs half the time.

But then that's all here in this journal.

I know I expected too much of her. I expected her to realize that despite the damn rejection letters I was a writer, a serious writer, that I had a writer's sensitivity and a writer's soul. I expected supportive. I expected quiet and gentle. From a New York City bitch born and bred, working her way up the ladder on Mad Ave and whose parents had left her oh, only about a million and a half.

I must have been out of my fucking mind.

I've got to remember not to expect too much from Cassie. Not right off the bat anyway. She could be ugly as a post for one thing. Despite the "long legs, green eyes, hot in a bathing suit" stuff. Green eyes do not a face make, right? But somehow I think her looks aren't going to matter to me all that much. She's the first one who's touched me in so long, who's really cared about me. And somehow I think she's what I guess you'd call a "real woman." With a real woman's wisdom. Not like Laura, who turned out in the end to be a spoiled little girl when you get right down to it. Who couldn't put up with the real Andrew Sky, occasional temper-tantrum and all.

But I've got to admit, I'm a little scared.

I've got a lot riding on this.

It may be that Cassie's my last hope for any real happiness on this earth. It's possible.

I'm not getting any younger after all. I smoke too much and probably I drink too much. I've only got twenty-five grand or so in the bank. I'm not bad looking but I'm no fucking Tom Cruise either.

She cares for me, though. I know that through her e-mails. So I've got reason to hope that my looks and all the rest of it won't mean any more to her than hers will to me. She seems to see right down into my soul sometimes. And that's an amazing thing, an amazing feeling. I might be driving off in a little while to meet my entire future. I'm scared, but shit, I'm excited too now. Writing this helped....and damn! it's filled the whole hour!

Jesus! I'd better get going. Better hit the road.

FROM THE DIARY OF CASSIE HOGAN

He's coming! Andrew's really coming to see me! ME!! I'm so excited. I can't sleep...I just had to get out of bed and write this down or I'll burst!!!

Mom's been a bitch all night. First she yelled at me about doing my homework...like I'll need to know Geometry... then she told me she made "arrangements" for me to stay with Aunt Kay while they're in Hawaii! No way.

What does she think I am? A baby?

I hate her! She'll be sorry when they get back and find out I left to be with Andrew. I'm not even going to leave them a note. Let them worry about what happened to me.

No. I can't do that to Daddy. I'll leave them a note and tell them the truth. That I love Andrew and we're going to get married and live happily ever after so they don't have to worry about me anymore. I'm a ~~big girl.~~ No...I'm a WOMAN.

I'm Andrew's woman. And he's my man. My love. My lover. I wonder if he'll want to "do it" when he gets here? If he does that's okay...because I found some of those things in Daddy's end-table and took one. A rubber. And my mother thinks I'm too young to stay by myself! Well, I'm old enough to know about rubbers, aren't I?

THE NET

I wonder if one will be enough?

Heather is going to be SO jealous!!! She thinks she's so hot because she's dating that dork from the junior college... but HE'S only nineteen and Andrew's in his forties. He's a REAL man! And he's mine. He loves me...he said so. And I love him!

And he's really, really coming!

God, I'm so excited. I just wish I looked better!!! I tried to get mom to drive me to the mall so I could get a haircut—I HATE my hair—but she wouldn't. Said she had too much to do and that my hair is fine the way it is. The BITCH! I wanted my hair to be perfect for Andrew but now it's just—UGH!

But I know my face will be okay. I took some of The Bitch's facial mask and scrub and used it on those stupid pimples on my chin. They're all red now but I think they'll be okay by morning. If they aren't I'll die! I'll kill myself if they aren't! Because Andrew deserves the best...and I want to be the best for him. I love him! And he loves me! But I'll still die if those pimples aren't better!!!

But really, I know he won't care about my hair or my skin. He loves me. The real me inside. Just like I love the real him inside.

I'm going to SURPRISE him! I'm going to wear my red nightgown when I open the door! That will REALLY make him happy!

I'll do anything to make him happy because I love him and his cat died.

Maybe we can go to the pet store after we do it and buy a kitten! I would just LOVE that!

God, I'm so nervous. I know I won't be able to sleep, but I have to. I HAVE to so I'll look good for Andrew. G'night, Dear Diary. I'll tell you all about it tomorrow...when Andrew comes for me!

SHINING IN THE DARK

TRANSCRIPT OF AN INTERVIEW GIVEN BY ANDREW J. SKY, OF 233 WEST 73RD STREET, N.Y., N.Y., WITNESSED BY LT. DONALD SEBALD, WARMINSTER P.D., 5/16/03

SKY: So I'm late because of this goddamn tire blowing out on me so a trip that should have taken me what? an hour and a half? took me about two and a half so I'm nervous, right? Nervous about meeting her and nervous about being late and I'm also filthy from changing the tire, anyhow I finally find the place in the dark and I ring the bell and she comes to the door wearing that little...

SEBALD: The red nightgown.

SKY: Yeah, and well, you know, she's not leaving a whole lot to the imagination and she's really pretty as hell but I can tell right away she's not happy to see me. I mean, there's no hugs or kisses or anything like in the e-mails and she's kind of frowning but damned if I know why. I'm not that ugly and I'm not that dirty and I'm dressed okay. Anyhow, she invites me in and asks if I want something to drink and I tell her I could sure use a beer and I tell her about the flat and ask could I wash up somewhere so she points me to the bathroom and I do. When I come out she's lightened up a bit and there's a beer open for me and a Pepsi for her and we're both on the couch in the living room only she's way over to one side while I'm over on the other and I'm wondering, why the frost? and it's making me even more nervous so I figure, you better just go ahead and ask her so that's what I do.

SEBALD: You ask her what, exactly?

SKY: I ask her what's wrong. She says she's been waiting for me all day. Like we'd set some specific time.

SEBALD: And you hadn't?

SKY: No, never. I don't know what she expected, that I was going to be there first thing in the morning or something so I tell her that. That I'm really sorry but that it was just a misunderstanding because we really hadn't set a particular time but I'm really, really sorry and that's when she tells me she didn't even go to school today, she stayed home waiting for me and that's when I start looking at her. I mean really looking at her. Up close, y'know? I guess I'd been afraid to do that before. I guess I was too fucking nervous at first and then there was all that frost. That plus the nightgown. But anyway, I look at her and realize that there's hardly a line on her face. Hardly a single line. I mean, I knew she was young, that was obvious right away. But still I figure, got to be college she's talking about. She skipped classes today waiting for me and I feel real bad about that so I tell her but jesus! then all of a sudden she's about to cry! I can't believe it! And I feel like, I don't know, I feel like I've probably fucked up again. Just by being late. Even though I'm not late. Not really. But then she stands up and says, come on, I want to show you something so I do, I follow her, and she walks me into her bedroom.

SEBALD: She leads you in? Of her own volition? That's what you're saying?

SKY: That's right. Of course of her own volition. And the first thing I notice, the first thing that anybody would notice is that this is a bedroom, right? And now I'm confused. I mean, she's just met me for the first time and she's damn near crying and she's led me right into her fucking bedroom! There's the bed, and there are all these posters on the wall, rock stars and movie stars and whatever, and there's her desk with the computer. And I'm looking at all this. Taking it in. But she's not interested in what I'm doing. She's pointing down beside the bed and she's got two suitcases there, sitting on the floor and she says look at that. So I ask her, suitcases? And she says I was going to run away with you tonight, you know that? Something like that, anyway, I don't remember exactly because by now I'm barely listening to her. It's like this whole thing is washing over me finally. I'm finally beginning to get it.

SEBALD: Get what?

SKY: The posters, the goddamn pennants on the walls. The teddy bears on the shelves over her desk. The photos on the mirror. She's a kid! She's a goddamn fucking kid! So I ask her. I get myself under control and I say, Cassie, exactly how old are you? And she says something like old enough and now she's crying for real but I don't give a damn, I'm having all I can do to stay calm enough to ask her one more time but I do, I ask her how fucking old, Cassie? And she says fifteen. Just like that. Fifteen! Defiant, like. Can you believe it? She's jailbait! All this time she's been conning me! Leading me on! I can show you the goddamn e-mails for chrissake! And now she wants to run away with me? Is she out of her fucking mind? Shit! Fuck!

SEBALD: Take it easy, Mr. Sky. Unless you want those cuffs again. Just go on telling us what happened.

SKY: Sorry. I'm sorry. It's just that…never mind. I just… jesus, I guess I just lost it at that point, you know? Went ballistic I guess. I grabbed her and slapped her and told her what I thought of her, called her a stupid little bitch, and she's crying, really going at it, and I remember grabbing her by the arm and throwing her across the bed so hard she fell all the way over to the floor on the other side. Then I trashed the room.

SEBALD: Trashed the room. Be explicit, please, for the record.

SKY: Tore down the posters, the pennants, broke the mirror with my fist, which is where these cuts come from, kicked in the full-length mirror on the door, knocked all the cosmetics and whatever shit she had there off her dresser and the dolls and bears off the shelf, tore up books, papers, whatever. (Pause.)

SEBALD: Go on, Mr. Sky. And where was she all this time?

SKY: She'd gotten up. She was standing on the far side of the bed and she was screaming for me to stop, she had a little cut on her forehead and I remember her face was all streaked and red from the crying. But she stayed right there yelling at me. Right up until I went for the computer. It was the computer, I guess, that did it for both of us. It was our link, you know? For me it meant one thing. For her I guess it meant another. But it was our link. Like a totem. She came at me as soon as I tore the wire off the mouse.

SEBALD: You're saying she came at you?

SKY: I guess she was trying to protect the computer. She kept calling me a bastard. I'm not a bastard. I was in love with her. Anyhow, before she made it around the bed I'd kicked in the side of the printer and by the time she actually reached me I'd torn the keyboard loose and I hit her with that, swung it at the side of her head.

SEBALD: Left side or right side?

SKY: What? Oh, left side, over the ear. And she went right down. Hit the floor at the foot of the bed, you know? Kneeling there, her arms on the bed, bleeding a little onto the bed, her legs curled under her on the floor.

SEBALD: She was alive then?

SKY: Oh yeah, she was alive. But she wasn't cursing at me anymore. She just sat there staring at me like I was dogshit, like I was the lowest thing she'd ever seen. And like she was afraid of me too, you know? Both things together. And I'd only seen that one other time on one other face, that combination I guess you'd say. On my ex. My girlfriend Laura. That she was scared of me and disgusted with me at the same time. So that was when I tore loose the monitor and used it on her. (Pause.)

SEBALD: Mr. Sky?

SKY: She loved that computer. So believe me, it wasn't easy.

THE NOVEL
OF THE HOLOCAUST

BY STEWART O'NAN

THE NOVEL OF the Holocaust is coming! Yessiree—alive, alive, alive! SEE the freak of the twentieth century, the soul-searching survivor of the ultimate battle of good and evil! HEAR his pitiful story of torture and degradation! THRILL to the savage, inhuman acts of his captors! Yes, he's coming, one command performance only, the sideshow setting up its tent in the meadow by the river. All day children have been racing their bikes across the bridge, fighting to peek under the canvas. Come one, come all!

No, it's not that bad, the Novel of the Holocaust thinks. But close. He's been chosen by Oprah, lifted up, summoned, so he's going. He leaves his walk-up in London while fog still hangs over Leicester Square, drenching the statues, the pigeons jabbing at his new shoes, bought just for this trip. He's got money now, and a famous name (though no face). He takes a taxi to Gatwick and pauses at the duty-free, the bottles of Scotch like parting gifts.

Irony is never lost on the Novel of the Holocaust. He grins at practically anything, yet is never more than amused. The Novel of the Holocaust is sober, and dresses well. If he should laugh out loud, people would turn and stare, as at a crazy old lady. Walking through the airport, the Novel of the Holocaust talks to himself, remembering storefronts and round, growling buses, letters in precise handwriting—the age that passed while he was waking up, shrugging off the losses of his boyhood. Now he is being celebrated for them. Waiting at the gate, he stops watching the miniature, repeating news and stares at his hands, wonders if this trip is worthwhile. He is used to a quiet life, his feelings for the world buried in his writing. Flying makes him nervous, and when the Novel of the Holocaust uses the restroom, he washes his hands before and after, alert for germs.

Of course the Novel of the Holocaust is nostalgic and melancholy, struck dumb by so many families parting as the plane boards. Children cling to their mothers' necks and scream until the grandparents haul them off, make them wave goodbye. The Novel of the Holocaust doesn't approve.

First class is new to him, a mark of how his stock has risen—utterly inexplicable, the result of a few phone calls. It's like Hollywood, he thinks; one day he's a starlet, the next a star. The screen at the front of the cabin shows the soft arc they're traveling, and their speed, the temperature outside (minus 500). The hours to New York tick off like a bomb. The Novel of the Holocaust can't sleep in his seat, drifts off to wake abruptly, his face falling forward.

The Novel of the Holocaust comes from an island with a view of a rocky shore, huts, goats tinkling as they navigate steep paths. The country people are simple and wise as mud. Until this, they considered The Novel of the Holocaust a failure, a child who knew too much and did too little.

The Novel of the Holocaust has no brothers or sisters, no wife or husband, no children, only lovers, and those are inconstant, staying a week on their way to Greece or the Middle East. They see the Novel of the Holocaust as harmless and a little outdated, good-hearted but hardly charming, the devotion he instills lukewarm. A friend, they say; I'm staying with a friend. The Novel of the Holocaust makes them breakfast and sees them downstairs to the taxi in the rain. He holds an umbrella, helps with the door, kisses them meagerly through the window, then climbs back up to the flat, gray in the morning light, the radiators hissing. The Novel of the Holocaust has the whole day and no plans.

Sometimes the Novel of the Holocaust goes to museums, hoping to meet people. Sometimes the Novel of the Holocaust doesn't leave the flat for a week, reads the paper cover to cover, flips on BBC 3 and lies on the couch, watching Antonioni, falling asleep. Sometimes the Novel of the Holocaust closes his eyes in the bathtub and sinks under, his thin hair lifting like kelp, and imagines a stranger's hand lurking above the surface, waiting to push his head down again.

Maybe fame will change the Novel of the Holocaust. The money is unimportant, but maybe people will see him differently. There will be fan letters, perhaps, or even fans themselves ringing the bell—girls at university and lunatics drawn by the controversy, crabbed scholars ready to dispute obscure points.

In the Novel of the Holocaust, the hero is a teenager named Franz Ignaz. Franz Ignaz comes from a city without goats and mud and his parents think he's wonderful. Franz Ignaz is a musical prodigy, a violinist since the age of four, an unsurpassed interpreter of Moscheles and Mendelssohn. In the shaking candlelit basement of a safe house, he plays their banned works for families on the run from the Gestapo.

The Novel of the Holocaust took piano lessons at public school but quit in the middle of Czerny's exercises. His teacher said he had a passable sense of meter, but no real ear. To truly play, he said, you have to start much younger, and how could the

Novel of the Holocaust explain his parents' house, the damp of the sea and the one shelf of wrinkled encyclopedias he read over and over? How could he say he was a dull child, and clumsy, always doing the wrong thing and then getting yelled at?

In the Novel of the Holocaust, the families can't applaud Franz Ignaz without giving themselves away, so they each touch his cheek, look into his eyes as a way of saying thanks. Later, in the camps, the same gesture is heartrending, and then brutal, when the commandant uses it. The Novel of the Holocaust's mother did the same thing when the Novel of the Holocaust had disappointed her or done something wrong (which was all the time). He tried to avoid her eyes, because they shamed him, and she took her hand and placed it on the side of his face and turned him toward her and then looked directly into him, and he could not keep his secrets. How this became such a large part of the book, the Novel of the Holocaust isn't sure, and what exactly it means escapes him. Guilt, certainly, or maybe an accusation against her, but when he thinks of his mother, she is blameless. Certainly she has nothing to do with the six million dead, and to compare his lonely childhood to genocide is an affront, an obscenity. But that is what he's done.

The flight attendants come around with hot towels, and the Novel of the Holocaust daubs his face with the lemony scent. After seven hours sitting, this is supposed to refresh him. He is supposed to be on an important morning show in less than an hour and he needs to figure out what he wants to say.

They will ask him about his parents—obliterated, like the island village, the goats roaming wild in the mountains, sleeping in the kitchens. They will say the magic name of the camp he survived as a child (no, he will not let them film the number bled green and near-indecipherable on his arm) and ask him to tell his story.

"In the book," he will say, bringing everything back to Franz Ignaz and Mendelssohn. He will champion Moscheles, a composer few know, and while this tactic will siphon off some time, it will not save him from his own story, the lines and insane paperwork separating the useful from the dead. He was a country boy, used to work, his calves bulging from climbing the switchbacked paths. His parents were old (though, as he explains this to himself, he realizes they were ten years younger than he is now). It is not a story that interests the Novel of the Holocaust. It was just bad luck, and that is not what the book is about.

Because the Novel of the Holocaust is magical. In the Novel of the Holocaust, Franz Ignaz meets a friend in the camps, a chess prodigy named David. David is eight and on the verge of becoming a grandmaster; his father and his father's father were champions in Breslau. This is not far from the truth, though the Novel of the Holocaust never met the boy, who was actually from another barracks. He was Latvian and his name started with a K. Kolya? He should remember. In real life, the boy was machinegunned with several hundred other children, but in the Novel of the Holocaust, he and Franz Ignaz have long talks about the logic of the Nazis, and how, by teasing out the metaphysical flaw in their rationalism, they can save everyone. Obviously this is comic, and while this reasoning didn't obtain in the real world of the camps, it holds a deeply human and philosophical truth that works brilliantly in the Novel of the Holocaust.

They're coming down into New York now, Long Island beside them most of the approach. The Novel of the Holocaust's ears pop unevenly, and he has to dig a pinkie into one. When the plane touches down, his neighbors applaud, and he thinks: Why?

The media escort from his American publishers is waiting for him at the gate, his book held up so he can recognize her. She wants to take his carry-on but he defeats her easily. Outside, the network limo is his, a leather cavern of a backseat complete with a bar, a TV tuned—permanently, he supposes—to the station he will be on.

"How's the tour going?" his escort asks, and he explains that this is his first stop, that usually he dreads these things, that he rarely leaves his apartment. He realizes how pathetic this sounds, even if it is true. Why does he feel the need to confess to strangers?

"You must be thrilled with the Oprah thing. We are."

"It was quite a surprise," he admits. "I must confess I don't know much about the show." "It's great," she assures him. "Everyone watches it."

Queens is flying by, and suddenly the Novel of the Holocaust is ravenously hungry. He would like to go to the hotel and sleep. Already he misses London, the view of the park from the tall windows, his kettle whistling on the burner, calling him away from the table, drawing him back again, briefly, into the real world.

A cemetery a mile long slides by, hills dotted with crosses—how many thousand?—and then the city rises in front of him like a fence, the river blue beneath them. He has been here before, a guest of his publishers, but never as a celebrity (though, oddly, he feels even less real now, more of an imposter). From the bridge, the facades glint prettily in the orange morning light, and the city seems his. He wonders if this is how power feels.

How many people live here—ten, twelve million? The Novel of the Holocaust imagines the dead taking their places, the apartments and office buildings filled with them, elevators hopelessly trying to close their doors.

It's a hazard of the profession, he thinks, or is it just his life, the fact that he was lucky (unlucky) enough to survive? He's here, the Novel of the Holocaust, about to be beamed across the United States, and he needs to be wise. The responsibility is impossible. What in the world can he say to these people?

They will want to talk about the movie, whether he's happy with the director (no) or with the script, a quilt of the simplest clichés. They will ask if the movie will be faithful to the book. Contractually, he is free to speak his mind, but his agent has counseled him to either say nice things or be pleasantly non-committal, take the question to the next abstract level of literature versus popular art.

In the movie of the Novel of the Holocaust, there are love scenes in the bunks. Franz Ignaz and David are teenagers, and both are in love with the same girl, who in the book is mentioned only twice. The Nazis will all be played by British actors, and the boys by two American TV stars. The director has decided the whole thing should take place in the summer, for a more striking contrast—birdsong and sun through the trees. He sees them using klezmer music for the village scenes and a brooding symphonic score for the camps. (Would, perhaps, Mendelssohn be appropriate? the Novel of the Holocaust wanted to ask.) All of this the director included in a long, episodic letter a month after he signed on to the project. The Novel of the Holocaust hasn't heard from him since, only vague updates from his agent.

"Would you sign my copy for me?" his escort asks, and automatically he takes the book from her, finds the title page and crosses out his name. This is what he is here to do.

"Thanks," she says. "I haven't actually had a chance to read it yet, but it looks interesting. I really liked Sophie's Choice."

"Never read it," he says, getting her back, but she trumps him, telling him he should see the movie, that Meryl Streep is really good in it.

They're into Manhattan now, traffic nosing light to light, the sidewalks mobbed. All dead, he thinks, pictures them all falling, bodies slumped over the steering wheels. Maybe then they would understand.

That's what he'll tell them! Imagine everyone in the city dead, the doormen and the matrons walking their dogs, the bicycle messengers.

What a pleasant guest he'll be.

On the way to the studio in midtown they pass a hundred coffee shops. A man on one corner is eating some kind of sandwich, and it is all the Novel of the Holocaust can do to keep from leaping out and snatching it from him, stuffing it in his mouth with greasy fingers.

"Can we stop and pick up something to eat?" he asks, but there's no time.

"They'll have a platter of something in the green room," she assures him, and they do, a tray of uncut bagels and squeeze packets of cream cheese. The coffee tastes like varnish. Someone with the show takes his arm and whisks him away to make-up, where he sits in a barber's chair before a mirror. The woman working on him says nothing; she's busy talking to another woman about her hours, how she wants to trade her shift with someone. The Novel of the Holocaust sits there with the bib protecting his suit, looking at the powdered and rouged old whore before him. It was all so long ago, he thinks, but that is not what they want to hear. And honestly, that is not true, not true at all.

They will ask him about the research, the crumbling files and filmy carbons he parsed, the thousands of pictures in the British Museum—all the while flipping those images like a narrated slide show. In the Novel of the Holocaust, Franz Ignaz tries to find out what happened to all the people in his apartment building. With the help of David and a kapo, he tracks them all down, and soon, after trading favors and paying off the right people, they're reunited—reconstituted into one barracks, a community again. They pretend they're still living in Danzig. The camp and what's happening lead them to believe in this, a kind of mass hallucination that helps keep their family intact.

Of course, the last people Franz Ignaz finds are his own mother and father, starving and doomed to a work detail. Once they are no longer useful, they will be killed, so Franz Ignaz must find a way to smuggle them food.

Did the Novel of the Holocaust ever have a chance to help his own mother and father? Would he rather have died with them? These are the old questions, maybe the ones the book was supposed to answer. But of course, it couldn't. It was just a book.

"You're done," the woman says, unclipping the bib, and he's lead back to the green room, where an athlete of some sort and his escort have taken his space on the couch.

"Two minutes," a man with a headset says to the Novel of the Holocaust's escort, and she asks permission before adjusting his tie and brushing the shoulders of his suit.

"You look gorgeous," she says, as if they're sharing a joke.

The man with the headset leads them down a hallway and carefully into a bright studio, gently closing the door behind them. The set is smaller than the Novel of the Holocaust thought, and raised, like a float in a parade. Another guest is on under the lights, a blonde woman taller than him, dressed to show off her strong arms and generous chest—a movie star. He wishes he knew who she is.

In real life, the Novel of the Holocaust never searched for his parents. He did not find anyone from his village. They were dead, everyone agreed, and though he did not believe it for several months, he had little else to occupy his mind, and too soon he accepted the truth. There were no miraculous escapes, no easy miracles. There was nothing funny or uplifting, no blackly operatic metaphors. He did not hide jewels to trade for favors or share his food with sickly children, and once they were liberated, he did not want to remember any of it.

He doesn't want to now, but at this point there's no choice. They're ready for him. The blonde is finished, and the man with the headset leads him to her chair, still warm from her. A sound man snakes a wire up through the front of his shirt, chilly against his skin, as the hostess thanks him for being on the show. She has so much make-up on that her face is divided into zones of color, a living Mondrian.

"I'm so honored to meet you. Your book is absolutely marvelous, truly heartbreaking."

He thanks her, nodding like a professor while the sound-man fiddles with his lapel. "Can we get a level?" a voice calls Godlike from the ceiling.

"Say something," the soundman orders.

"Hello," the Novel of the Holocaust says. "Can you hear me?"

"That's fine," the ceiling replies.

"Thirty seconds," the man with the headset says.

The Novel of the Holocaust's escort stands offstage by the door with her copy, giving him a thumbs-up.

"I'm going to introduce you and the book and then I'll ask you a few questions," the hostess says. "Don't worry, it'll be over before you know it."

He thinks of London again, his computer waiting on the table, the kitchen empty, the post piling up. How quiet it must be, how still. Why does this seem ideal to him, the best way to spend his days?

In real life, everyone he knew as a child died. The soldiers came with their boats and took everyone away and killed them one by one, and only he survived. That is the secret of the Novel of the Holocaust, one he has told nobody, and never will, not now, not ever (oh, but don't they know?). In the Novel of the Holocaust, the people he loves live forever. For that lie, he is being made famous.

"Five, four," the man with the headset says, and finishes the countdown with his fingers.

"We're back," the hostess says, leaning toward the camera, and introduces him, telling the country he's written a luminous, important book about the darkest tragedy of our time which Oprah Winfrey has just chosen for her book club, and that he's flown in directly from London, England just to be on today's show. She turns to him, connects with his eyes, and he can't help but picture his mother, her hand on his cheek. What would she think?

"Thank you so much for visiting with us this morning."

"Thank you," the Novel of the Holocaust says. "I'm glad to be here."

AELIANA

BY BEV VINCENT

THE SUN HAS been down for nearly an hour when Aeliana emerges from her lair in the basement of an abandoned building located at the far end of a dark alley in a seedy corner of a dismal city. Even this dank cavern does not provide complete protection, for there are filthy, cracked windows at the top of the wall that admit sunlight, so Aeliana has constructed a secondary shelter using scraps of cardboard, wood and metal scavenged from the streets above.

She loves being outside when the moon is high, exploring the world while foraging for food. She isn't fussy. If she doesn't beat the rats to the choicest tidbits in the garbage barrels, there are always the rats themselves.

Stored heat from the daylight hours radiates from the concrete and asphalt. Her sensitive nose picks up a scent. The remains of someone's partially digested meal are splattered on the pavement next to a supine body, but the man is still warm and breathing, so she leaves him alone. Most of the humans she encounters at night are dead. Around here, life is both short and cheap.

When she creeps around the corner, she detects a new odor riding on the stagnant air: fresh meat. A naked body is sprawled face down in the middle of the alley. Arms spread, nose crushed into the pavement. Dead a few hours, Aeliana estimates.

She associates discoveries like this with the man she calls the Lord of the Dusk. He comes during the grey minutes between daytime and night, and he always leaves behind a body. Her lair is littered with the bones of men and women such as these. They seem almost like gifts left expressly for her.

As Aeliana draws nearer, something squeals behind her. Flashing lights paint the alley red, then blue, then red again. Car doors open. Feet approach. Aeliana darts into the shadows, presses herself against the wall and holds her breath.

"Over here," a man's voice says.

A flashlight beam plays across the alley, passing over Aeliana's furry paws. She tucks them under her body and cowers.

"I'll call it in," a woman says.

The beam finds Aeliana once more. "The fuck?" the man says. "Emerson, do you see this?"

In the poor light, Aeliana might be mistaken for a lynx in her current form. However, upon closer inspection, her eyes are too large and expressive, her features too broad. Her talons are too long and limber for a feline and her hair too wispy. She has seen herself through the eyes of humans, and understands how they perceive her. Weird, hideous, obscene.

Aeliana tries to escape the beam, but it stays on her. It doesn't hurt—not like sunlight—but she's exposed and defenseless. Every predator is also prey to something else.

The man removes a weapon from his holster and takes aim.

Aeliana knows about guns. Many of her kind have been wounded or killed over the ages. She leaps just as he fires. The bullet misses—barely—but a splinter of brick from the wall slashes her hind paw.

Ignoring the pain, she darts down the alley in search of the sanctuary of darkness. The man does not shoot a second time. After she turns the corner, she limps toward her refuge. She pushes the door closed behind her and stumbles down the wooden stairs. She collapses, panting, at the bottom. The basement floor is cold and unyielding, but she feels safe here.

She closes her eyes. A golden glow envelops her as she returns to human form. She resembles a child of perhaps twelve, but she is far older than that. She will probably never look like an adult, no matter how many years pass.

The injury to her paw becomes a sizeable gash on her foot. It will heal with time, but for now it hurts. Besides the pain, she's hungry. The unpleasant encounter robbed her of her chance to feast. In a few hours, once the outsiders have gone away, she'll try again. Being injured will make her more vulnerable, but it's a risk she'll have to take.

She crawls across the rough floor to the pile of clothes near the entrance to her lair. After dressing, she finds a scrap of cloth long enough to wrap around the wound on her foot.

A light flashes across the grime-covered windows at the top of the basement wall. She hears a scuffling noise. Another flash of light. Then she hears the distinctive squeak of the hinges as the door above swings inward.

Someone's coming.

Officer Kate Emerson's heavy duty flashlight picks up the splashes of red leading down the alley. She's the senior partner, so she leaves Philips to preserve the crime scene and wait for backup while she follows the trail. Her sidearm is still holstered, but the flap is unsnapped for quick access.

Philips thinks he saw a wildcat, but the darkness can play tricks on a person. If it was the killer who has been dumping bodies in this part of town for the past several months, she can't let him get away. Catching this perp will look very good on her record—another step up the ladder toward a gold shield, bumping her pay and getting her off the streets at night. A detective's life is less dangerous, and she has a little girl at home without a father.

The trail leads around the corner to a wooden door at the end of the next alley. Three drops of wet blood on the sill gleam in her flashlight beam. She considers radioing Philips, but he'll only tell her to wait for backup. That would be the by-the-book thing to do, but she doesn't want the killer to escape.

She puts her hand on the doorknob and twists. The door swings open. The hinges utter a loud protest. So much for sneaking up on whomever or whatever Philips wounded.

The dirt on the floor in the entrance is undisturbed, but she finds tracks on the basement stairs to the right. Recent, from the look of them. If they're paw prints, they're unlike any she's ever seen. She also finds a drop of blood on the second step. As she descends, she unholsters her pistol and extends it, bracing her gun arm with the one holding the flashlight.

Once she reaches the basement, she sees signs that something was dragged—or has dragged itself—across the filthy concrete floor. More blood, too. She takes a few cautious steps forward, sweeping the area with her flashlight. The basement is littered with trash. In one corner she sees what might be a stack of bleached bones. Is this the killer's lair?

Her flashlight makes her an easy target, but she'd be more vulnerable in the dark. Moving forward, she sees something that looks like a hovel or a lean-to. Then she sees a flash of color and swings the flashlight—and her gun—a few inches to her left.

She gasps and eases the pressure on the trigger. It's a little girl, crouching like a leopard ready to pounce. Ten years old, maybe a little older. Her mane of curly golden hair looks like it hasn't seen a brush in...forever. She's dressed in tattered, filthy rags.

"What are you doing down here?" Before holstering her sidearm, she looks beyond the child to see if there's anyone else in the shelter. "Where are your mommy and daddy?"

The girl stands, but remains mute.

Emerson steps closer. Her beam washes over the girl from head to toe. She's barefoot. A makeshift bandage on her right foot is oozing blood.

"Let me take a look at that."

The girl doesn't move.

"I won't hurt you. I just want to look at your foot."

The girl shakes her head.

Emerson kneels to make herself less threatening. After a few seconds, the girl limps across the basement floor.

"What's your name?" Emerson asks. She's unprepared for what happens next. Her thoughts are flooded with a name that announces itself inside her head so loud it might have been delivered by a concert hall PA system. She reels, putting out a hand to keep from falling over.

After taking a deep breath, she looks at the girl. She reminds Emerson of one of those kitschy paintings of little waifs with oversized eyes. Her grime-covered face is somber, as if she's lived a life of sorrow and torment.

"Did you do that? Are you Aeliana?"

The girl nods. A hint of a smile curls her lips. She rocks from one foot to the other and then grimaces in pain.

"Pleased to meet you. I'm Kate." Emerson pats her bent leg, guiding the girl over to the makeshift seat. She wraps one arm around Aeliana's waist and picks her up, clutching her to her chest. She pivots and heads toward the basement steps. "Don't worry," she says. "I'll take you somewhere safe."

The girl squirms, forcing Emerson to use both hands to maintain control. The flashlight traces an erratic tattoo on the walls and ceiling as it tumbles to the ground.

An unusual, bitter odor envelops Emerson. The frail body clasped in her arms feels like it's melting away to nothing. A wave of heat rolls over her and something flows down her body, as if a bucket of lukewarm water has been poured on her. After a few seconds, her arms are pressing against her breasts. She's an experienced cop who knows how to restrain perps, but somehow this little girl has managed to escape her grasp. Taking deep breaths to maintain her composure, she fights the urge to turn and flee. It's just a little girl, she tells herself. A frightened, injured girl. And it's her duty to protect her.

She picks up the flashlight, which survived its fall to the cement floor. The beam illuminates Aeliana, who is crouching in front of her hovel again, like a feral animal. For a few seconds it seems like her features are shifting. Her nose narrows and her broad forehead flattens. Emerson tells herself it's a trick of the shadows and light, because now Aeliana looks just like a little girl.

"Will you stay here until I come back with something to take care of your foot?" she asks. "I won't try to take you away again."

Aeliana nods.

"Was that your daddy? In the alley?" Emerson's head jerks back when a vivid mental image of the body imprints on her mind.

Aeliana shakes her head.

"Wow. Okay. And what about your mommy?"

The girl shrugs.

Emerson doesn't know how to process the things that have happened since she arrived in the basement. All she can do is take care of the girl's injuries. For now, at least. "I'll be right back," she says. "Stay here."

She's halfway up the stairs when her radio crackles on her shoulder. "Emerson? You there?"

"I lost the trail. I'm on my way back to you now."

"Reinforcements are five minutes out," he says.

"Roger," she says.

The crime scene turns into a beehive of activity. In her absence, Philips strung yellow tape to keep all but essential personnel from the area. CSI techs erect lights and begin the arduous task of collecting evidence. The detectives who take over the scene send Emerson and Philips to canvass the neighborhood for witnesses. It's busywork—no one around here would ever talk to the cops about anything—but it's part of the job.

Philips takes the east side of the alley and Emerson the west. Before she heads out, she removes some first aid supplies and other items from the trunk of their squad car. She makes a show of knocking on doors and then, at the first opportunity, disappears around the corner.

Aeliana emerges from the shanty in the basement when Emerson reaches the bottom step. Emerson shows her the supplies. "I promise," she says. "I won't try to take you away again."

The girl approaches slowly but eventually agrees to sit on Emerson's lap again while the officer cleans the wound, applies ointment and wraps the foot with a gauze bandage. "Try to keep it clean," Emerson says. "Are you hungry?"

The girl nods.

Emerson hands over the turkey salad sandwich that was supposed to be her lunch. She twists the cap on a bottle of water before passing it over, too. "Do you know anything about the man in the alley?"

A scene plays out in Emerson's head, like an old news reel. The perspective is unusual, low to the ground. A car tire rolls to a stop at the entrance to an alley. The door opens and a foot appears. The view pans up to show a man removing something heavy from the trunk. He carries it down the darkening alley, dumps it on the ground and returns to the car, which drives off a few seconds later.

"Did you see his face?"

Emerson receives an image of a man cloaked in shadows. She can make out a few features—prominent ears, receding hairline—but not enough to identify him.

"He's the Lord of the Dusk," Aeliana says, speaking out loud for the first time.

"Why do you call him that?" The media hasn't yet caught wind of the fact that someone is dropping bodies in this part of town—and no one cares enough to inform them—so the killer doesn't have a nickname.

"I am a disciple of the moon and the stars," Aeliana says, pointing at herself. "You are a daughter of the sun. He comes in between."

Emerson nods, even though she has no idea what Aeliana means.

"If I see him again, I can summon you."

"How?"

Another image floods Emerson's mind. Aeliana beckoning her.

"Can you do that wherever I am?"

Aeliana shrugs. "I think so."

"He's dangerous."

More images parade through Emerson's head. Hideous monsters with fangs and claws. She looks again at the little girl and tries to imagine what happened earlier when she melted out of her arms. Does she have an aspect like this, too? She understands the message, though. Aeliana is dangerous as well.

"Okay, but don't take any chances," she says. "Keep safe. I'll come back when I can."

Emerson brushes the tangled hair away from Aeliana's face and kisses her forehead. Once again she smells the unusual aroma. It reminds her of death.

AELIANA

Aeliana senses the Lord of the Dusk bringing a new present before she sees him. She closes her eyes and transmits a message to Kate. Their empathic connection is strong. She hasn't bonded with a human in a long, long time. Not only can she send Kate messages, she can see through her eyes and allow Kate to see through hers.

Kate has visited her three times since that first night, bringing food—some of it unlike anything Aeliana has ever experienced before—and tending to her wound, which is healing nicely. Each time she tried to convince Aeliana to go away with her. She has banished from her mind the images Aeliana showed her and thinks of Aeliana as a child.

Aeliana knows that what Kate wants is not possible. They are from two different worlds—worlds that must always remain apart.

It's early evening when Kate parks her car on the street near Aeliana's alley. From the safety of her enclosure, Aeliana sends her mind out into the foreign realm of daylight, as seen through Kate's eyes. She flinches at first, unaccustomed to the brightness.

"You're sure he's coming?" Kate thinks.

"Soon," Aeliana says. She looks to the sky through the car's windscreen, taking advantage of the rare opportunity to see the sun, which is about to disappear behind the city's sprawling skyline. Kate raises her hand to shield her eyes, which amuses Aeliana. Even humans aren't immune to its oppressive radiance.

They sit in comfortable silence for a while. Aeliana enjoys being inside Kate's mind. She has been alone for so long that it feels good to have company. She wanders through the woman's memories. Most of them involve a little girl—Kate's daughter. Aeliana feels like she's wrapped up in a warm blanket.

SHINING IN THE DARK

Emerson hears an approaching vehicle. The sun is now behind the skyscrapers. Shadows stretch into impossible lengths, distorting even the most familiar objects. She slumps behind the steering wheel as a car crawls past, going barely twenty. Once it's out of sight, she gets out and creeps down the street, sticking to the shadows. Aeliana approves.

Ahead, brake lights illuminate. The driver's door opens and a tall figure gets out. He puts his hands on the car roof as he surveys the area. Apparently satisfied that he's alone, he eases the door shut and walks to the back of the car. The trunk pops open. He reaches in and removes something large and cumbersome, dragging in toward the alley.

Emerson takes advantage of his distraction to ease closer. She has her gun out now, ready for the confrontation that will put an end to this killer's reign of terror. She should call this in, but she doesn't want to share the credit. Once she has the upper hand, she can make the call. It won't matter that she's off duty. Her bosses will lavish her with praise and the promise of promotion.

At the entrance to the alley, she braces herself and swings around the corner, gun at arm's length. "Freeze," she says in her loudest, sternest, most authoritative voice.

The man tackles her, knocking the gun from her hand. Something solid hits her head. She collapses. Then the man is on top of her slapping and punching. He pins her arms to her sides. Aeliana is screaming inside her head and Emerson thinks she's screaming out loud, too, but she can't be sure.

The man snarls. Emerson can't make out his words. They're the ravings of a maniac. Something pierces her belly. She looks down in time to see him pull out the knife and plunge it into her again. The pain is worse than when she was wounded in a shootout a few years ago. Her body goes cold, then hot, then cold again. Her attacker removes the knife and wipes it on her shoulder. Then she passes out.

AELIANA

A golden aura envelops Aeliana as she shifts into animal form. It's not quite dark outside yet, but she is driven by fury. Kate needs her help. She can already feel the woman's essence draining away.

Within seconds, she's bounding down the alley. The Lord of the Dusk is still leaning over Kate. He does not hear her approach. In a single leap she's on him. Her fangs find the soft meat of his neck and her claws dig into his back and arms. The knife clatters to the ground. He tries to reach for her, but she's too agile. Gouts of blood erupt from his neck. She closes her mouth, ripping off a huge piece of meat. Her molars grind it and she swallows.

The man collapses. Aeliana drags him away from Kate so his blood won't taint her. He isn't dead yet, but he won't last long.

She doesn't want Kate to see her like this, so she retreats into the shadows and shifts once more. The sun is almost gone, but she can still feel its diffuse rays singeing her flesh. She tugs on Kate's arm, trying to get her to wake up. Aeliana doesn't know how to staunch the flow of blood from the stab wounds in her abdomen.

Soon, it's dark and Aeliana is in her element. The man is dead, but Kate is still breathing, though her respiration is shallow and uneven. Her eyelids flutter open and she tries to focus on Aeliana. The little girl who isn't really a little girl.

"Get up," Aeliana says.

"Oof," Kate says when she tries to move. She puts a hand on her stomach. It comes away coated with blood. Something that should have been on her insides protrudes from one of the gaping wounds.

Aeliana flows into Kate's mind. Her thoughts are muddled. She's on the verge of passing out again. "Get up," Aeliana yells, both out loud and inside the woman's head.

"No use," Kate says.

Aeliana knows it's true. No one knows she's here. Even if an ambulance arrived this very minute, she's lost too much blood.

"No use." She shivers, and a tear rolls down her cheek. "My little girl," she says, and Aeliana, who is both beside Kate and inside her, understands that Kate isn't talking about her.

Kate's lungs are screaming for oxygen. She will die soon, and Aeliana can't take away her pain. Dying terrifies Kate, Aeliana realizes. For her, it's the end. Some of Aeliana's kind can go beyond death, but Kate can't.

As if Kate can hear Aeliana's thoughts, she turns toward her. "Change me. Make me eternal. Like you."

Aeliana shakes her head.

"Want to see...my little girl...grow up."

"I can't," she says.

"Please."

"You would have to leave your world behind."

"Don't...understand..."

"Your daughter would become as a dream to you." Aeliana doesn't add that Kate's daughter would also likely be repulsed by her.

"No." Pain wracks Kate's body. She can barely keep her eyes open. She stretches out a bloody hand toward the little girl at her side. "Melissa."

"I'll find her," Aeliana says.

She's still intertwined with Kate's mind when the woman dies. She's always wondered what it would be like. Someday, her turn might come. Or maybe she'll live forever.

It won't be long before the feral cats and rats and other vermin of the streets lay claim to the bodies in the alley. She wishes she could protect Kate from this indignity, but the world will have its way with her.

Aeliana turns to the other bodies, those of the murdered man and his killer, whose blood she has already tasted. She will feast on these remains before the scavengers arrive, and take enough with her to last for days. Eventually the men with the red and blue flashing lights will come and cart away what's left of them.

After that?

Aeliana isn't afraid of the future. Even without presents from the Lord of the Dusk, there will always be something to eat in this seedy corner of this dismal city.

PIDGIN AND THERESA

BY CLIVE BARKER

(PRESENTED IN ITS original British format.)

THE APOTHEOSIS OF Saint Raymond of Crouch End took place, as do the greater proportion of English exaltations, in January. Being a murky month, January is considered in celestial circles a wiser time to visit England than any other. A month earlier, and the eyes of children are turned heavenward in the hope of glimpsing reindeer and sleigh. A month later, and the possibility of spring—albeit frail—is enough to sharpen the senses of souls dulled by drear. Given that angels have a piquancy which may be nosed at a quarter-mile (likened by some to the smell of wet dog-fur and curdled cream) the less alert the populace the greater the chance that an act of divine intervention (such as the removal of a saint to glory) can be achieved without attracting undue attention.

So January it was. January 17, in fact; a Friday. A damp, cold, misty Friday; ideal circumstances for a discreet apotheosis. Raymond Pocock, the saint-to-be, lived in a pleasant but ill-lit street fully a quarter-mile from Crouch End's main thoroughfare, and given that by four in the afternoon the rain-clouds had conspired with dusk to drive all but the dregs of light from the sky, nobody even saw the angel Sophus Demdarita come calling.

Sophus was no naïf when it came to the business at hand. The child-healer Pocock would be the third soul she had removed from the hylic to the etheric conditions in a little over a year. But this afternoon there was error in the air. No sooner had she stepped into Raymond's squalid flat—intending to claim him silently—than his gaudy parrot, perched upon the window-sill, rose up shrieking in alarm. Pocock sluggishly attempted to hush it, but the bird's din had already set the occupants of the flat below and beside his yelling for some hush. When they didn't get it they came to the Saint's front door, threatening both bird and owner alike, and one—finding the door unlocked—threw it open.

Sophus was a pacifist. Though there were many amongst the Sublime Throng who enjoyed causing a little mayhem if they could get away with it, Sophus's father had been a legionnaire during the Purge of Dis, and had told his daughter such gruesome tales of those massacres that she could not now picture blood-letting of any sort without nausea. So instead of dispatching the witnesses at the door which would have solved so many problems—Sophus attempted to snatch Pocock from his sordid state with sufficient speed and light that those at the threshold would not believe what they had seen.

First she bathed the joyless room in such a blaze of beatific light that the witnesses were obliged to cover their eyes and retreat into the grimy hall. Then she embraced the good man Raymond and laid upon his forehead the kiss of canonization. At her touch his marrow evaporated and his flesh lost all but its spiritual weight. Finally, she lifted him up, dissolving with a glance the ceiling, beams and roof above them, and took him away into paradise.

The witnesses, speechless with confusion and fear, hurried away to their rooms and locked their doors to keep this wonder from coming in pursuit of them. The house grew still. The rain fell, and the night came with it.

In the Many Mansions Saint Raymond of Crouch End was received with much glory and rhetoric. He was bathed, dressed in raiments so fine they made him weep, and invited before the Throne to speak of his good deeds. When he protested mildly that it would he immodest for him to list his achievements, he was told that modesty had been invented by the Fallen One to encourage men to think less of themselves, and that he should have no fear of censure for his boasts.

Though it was less than an hour since he'd been sitting in his room composing a poem on the tragedy of flesh, that squalid state was already a decaying memory. Asked to recall the living creatures with whom he had shared that room, it is unlikely he would have been able to name them, and unlikelier still that he'd have recognized them now.

'Will you look at me?' the parrot said, peering at himself in the tiny mirror which had been the Saint's one concession to vanity. 'What the hell's happened?' His feathers lay in a bright pile beneath his perch. The flesh their shedding had revealed was scabby and tight, and it itched like the Devil, but he wasn't displeased. He had arms and legs. He had pudenda hanging in his belly's shadow that were impressively large. He had eyes in the front of his head, and a mouth (beneath a beakish nose) which made words that were not some babble recited by rote, but his own invention. 'I'm human,' he said. 'By Jesu, I'm human!'

He was not addressing an empty room. Sitting in the far corner, having first shed her shell and then swelled to four feet eleven, was the sometime tortoise Theresa, a gift to Raymond from a little girl who had been cured of a stammer by the Saint's tender ministrations.

'How did this happen?' the parrot, who'd been dubbed Pidgin by Raymond in recognition of its poor English, wanted to know.

Theresa raised her grey head. She was both bald and uncommonly ugly, her flesh as wrinkled and scaly in this new incarnation as ever it had been in her old. 'He was taken by an angel,' she said. 'And we were somehow altered by its presence. She stared down at her crabbed hands. 'I feel so naked,' she said. 'You are naked,' Pidgin replied. 'You've lost your shell and I've lost my feathers. But we've gained so much.' 'I wonder ...' Theresa said. 'What do you wonder?' 'Whether we've gained much at all.

Pidgin went to the window, and put his fingers on the cold glass. 'Oh, there's so much to see out there,' he murmured.

'It looks pretty miserable from here, 'God in Heaven—'

'Hold your tongue,' Theresa snapped. 'Somebody could be listening.'

'So?'

'Parrot, think! It wasn't the Lord's intention that we be transfigured this way. Are we agreed on that?'

'We are.'

'So if you raise your voice to Heaven, even in a casual curse, and someone up there hears your cry—'

'They may turn us back into animals?'

'Precisely.'

'Then we should get out of here as quickly as possible. Find ourselves some of Saint Raymond's clothes and go out into the world.'

Twenty minutes later they were standing on Crouch End, perusing a copy of the Evening Standard they'd plucked from a waste-bin. People hurried past them through the drizzle, scowling, muttering and pushing them as they passed. 'Are we in their way?' Theresa wanted to know. 'Is that the problem?' 'They just don't notice us, that's all. If I were standing here in my feathers—' 'you'd he locked up as a freak.' Theresa replied. She returned to the business of reading. 'Terrible things,' she sighed. 'Everywhere. Such terrible things.' She passed the paper over to Pidgin. 'Murdered children. Burning hotels. Bombs in toilet bowls. It's one atrocity after another. I think we should find ourselves some little island, where neither man nor angel will find us.' 'And turn our backs on all of this?' Pidgin said, spreading his arms and catching a young lady with his fingers. 'Watch your fucking hand,' she snarled, and hurried on. 'They don't notice us, huh?' Theresa said. 'I think they see us very well.' 'The rain has dampened their spirits,' Pidgin said. 'They'll brighten up once it clears.' 'You're an optimist, parrot,' Theresa murmured fretfully. 'And that could well be the death of you.' 'Why don't we find ourselves something to eat?' Pidgin suggested, taking hold of Theresa's arm. There was a supermarket a hundred yards from where they stood, its bright windows glittering in the puddled pavement. 'We look grotesque,' Theresa objected. 'They'll lynch us if they see us too clearly.' 'You're dressed badly, it's true,' Pidgin replied. 'I, on the other hand, bring a touch of glamour to my dress.' He had chosen from Raymond's wardrobe the best copy of his feathers he could find, but what upon his back had been a glorious display of natural beauty was now a motley of gaud and fat. As for Theresa, she too had found an approximation of her former state, heaping upon her spine enough thick coats and cardigans (all greys and greens) that she was bent almost double by their weight. 'I suppose if we keep to ourselves we might get away with our lives,' Theresa said. 'So do you want to go in or not?' Theresa shrugged. 'I am hungry.' she murmured. They furtively slipped inside and sloped up and down the aisles, choosing indulgences: biscuits, chocolates, nuts, carrots and a large bottle of the cherry brandy Raymond had been secretly addicted to since the previous September. Then they wandered up the hill and found themselves a bench outside Christchurch, close to the summit of Crouch End Hill. Though the trees around the building were bare, the mesh of their branches offered the wanderers some protection from the rain, and there they sat to nibble, drink and debate their freedom. 'I feel a great responsibility.' Theresa said. 'You do?' said Pidgin, claiming the brandy bottle from her scaly fingers. 'Why, exactly?' 'Isn't it obvious? We're walking proof of miracles. We saw a saint ascend—' 'and we saw his deeds,' Pidgin added. 'All those children, those pretty little girls, healed by his goodness. He was a great man.' 'They didn't enjoy the healing much, I think,' Theresa observed, 'they wept a lot.' 'They were cold, most likely. What with their being naked, and his hands being clammy.' 'And perhaps he was a little clumsy with his fingers. But he was a great man. Just as you say. Are you done with the brandy?' Pidgin handed the bottle—which was already half empty—back to his companion. 'I saw his fingers slip a good deal,' the parrot-man went on. 'Usually...' 'Usually?' '...well, now I think of it, always...' 'Always?' 'He was a great man.' 'Always?' 'Between the legs.' They sat in silence for a few moments, turning this over.

'You know what?' Theresa finally said

'What?' 'I suspect our Uncle Raymond was a filthy degenerate.' Another long silence. Pidgin stared up through the branches at the starless sky. 'What if they find him out?' 'That depends if you believe in Divine Forgiveness or not.' Theresa took another mouthful of brandy. 'Personally, I think we may not have seen the last of our Raymond.'

The Saint never knew what his error was; never knew whether it was an unseemly glance at a cherubim, or the way he sometimes stumbled on the word child that gave him away. He only knew that one moment he was keeping the company of luminous souls whose every step ignited stars, the next their bright faces were gazing upon him with rancour, and the air which had filled his breast with bliss had turned to birch twigs and was beating him bloody.

He begged for sympathy; begged and begged. His desires had overcome him, he admitted, but he had resisted them as best he could. And if on occasion he'd succumbed to a shameful fever, was that beyond forgiveness? In the grand scheme of things, he had surely done more good than bad.

The birches did not slow their tattoo by a beat. He was driven to his knees, sobbing. Let me go, he finally told the Sublime Throng, I relinquish my sainthood here and now. Punish me no more just send me home. The rain had stopped by eight forty-five, and by nine, when Sophus Demdarita brought Raymond back to his humble abode, the clouds were clearing. Moonlight washed the room where he'd healed half a hundred little girls, and where half a hundred times he'd sobbed in shame. It lit the puddles on the carpet, where the rain had poured through the gaping roof. It lit too the empty wooden box where his tortoise had lived, and the pile of feathers beneath Pidgin's perch. 'You bitch!' he said to the angel. 'What did you do to them?' 'Nothing,' Sophus replied. She already suspected the worst. 'Stay quite still or you'll confuse me.'

Fearing another beating. Raymond froze and as the angel frowned and murmured the empty air gave up ghosts of the past. Raymond saw himself, rising from his sonnets, as a syrup of hallowed light announced some heavenly presence. He saw the parrot fly up from its perch in alarm; saw the door thrown open as the neighbours came to complain and saw them retreat from the threshold in awe and terror.

The recollection grew frenetic now, as Sophus became more impatient to solve this mystery. The ethereal forms of angel and man rose through the roof, and Raymond turned his gaze upon the conjured images of Pidgin and Theresa. 'My God,' he said. 'What's happening to them?' The parrot was thrashing as if possessed, its plumage dropping out as its flesh swelled and seethed. The tortoise's shell cracked as she too grew larger, giving up her reptilian state for an anatomy that looked more human by the moment.

'What have I done?' Sophus murmured, 'God in Heaven, what have I done?' She turned on the sometime Saint. 'I blame you for this,' she said. 'You distracted me with your tears of gratitude. And now I'm obliged to do what I promised my father I would never do.'

'What's that?' 'Take a life,' Sophus replied, watching the speeding images closely. The parrot and the tortoise were stealing clothes, and making for the door. The angel followed. 'Not one life,' it said mournfully. 'Two. It must be as though this error was never made.'

The streets of north London are not known for miracles. Murder they had seen, and rape, and riot. But revelation? That was for High Holborn and Lambeth. True, there has been an entity with the body of a chow-chow and the head of Winston Churchill reported in Finsbury Park, but this unreliable account was the closest the region had come to having a visitation since the fifties.

Until tonight. Tonight, for the second time within the space of five hours, miraculous lights appeared, and on this occasion (the rain having passed, and the balmier air having coaxed revellers abroad) they did not go unnoticed.

Sophus was in too much of a hurry to be stealthy. She passed along the Broadway in the form of a hovering bonfire, startling atheists from their ease and frightening believers into catechisms. A stupefied solicitor, witnessing this fiery passage from his office window, called both the police and the fire department. By the time Sophus Demdarita was at the bottom of Crouch End Hill there were sirens in the air. 'I hear music,' said Theresa. 'You mean alarms.' 'I mean music.' She rose from the bench, bottle in hand, and turned towards the modest church behind them. From inside came the sound of a choir in full throat. 'What is it they're singing?' 'A Requiem,' Theresa replied, and started up the steps towards the church.

'Where the fuck are you going?' 'To listen,' Theresa said. 'At least leave me the...' He didn't get to the word brandy. The sirens had drawn his gaze back towards the bottom of the hill, and there, flooding the asphalt, he saw Sophus Demdarita's light. 'Theresa?' he murmured.

Getting no reply, he glanced back towards his companion. Unaware of their jeopardy, she was at the side porch, reaching open the door.

Pidgin yelled a warning—or at least tried to—but when he raised his voice something of the bird that he'd been surfaced, and the cry became a strangled squawk. Even if she had comprehended his words Theresa was deaf to them, transported by the Requiem's din. In a moment, she was gone from sight.

Pidgins first instinct was to run; to put as much distance as he could between his new-fangled flesh and the Angel that wanted to unmake him. But if he fled now, and the divine messenger did Theresa some fatal harm, what was left for him? A life lived in hiding, fearful of every light that passed his window; a life in which he dared not confess the miracle that had transformed him for fear some witless Christian divulged his whereabouts to God? That was a pitiful way to exist. Better to face the vile undoer now, with Theresa at his side.

He started up the steps with a bound, and the Angel, catching sight of him in the shadows, picked up its speed, ascending the hill at a run, its flaming body seeming to grow with every stride. Gasping with panic, Pidgin raced to the porch, flung open the door and stumbled inside.

A wave of melancholy came to greet him from the far end of the church, where perhaps sixty choristers were assembled in front of the altar, singing some song of death. Theresa glanced 'round at him, her dark eyes brimming with tears. 'Isn't it beautiful?' she said. 'The Angel.' 'Yes, I know. It's come for us,' she said, glancing back at the stained-glass window behind them, A fiery light was burning outside, and shafts of purple, blue and red fell around the fugitives. 'It's no use running. We're better off enjoying the music, until the end.'

The choir had not given up its Libera Me, despite the brightening blaze. Transported by the music, most of the singers continued to give of their best, believing perhaps that this glory was a glimpse of transcendence, induced by the Requiem. Instead of losing power, the music swelled as the doors at the back of the church swung open and Sophus Demdarita made her entrance.

The conductor, who until now had been blissfully unaware of what was afoot, glanced 'round. The baton fell from his fingers. The choir, suddenly unled, lost its way in the space of a bar, and the Requiem became a tattered cacophony from which the Angel's voice rose like the whine of a finger on the rim of a glass. 'You,' it said, pointing its finger at Pidgin and Theresa. 'Come here.' 'Tell it to fuck off,' Pidgin said to Theresa. 'Come to me!' "Theresa turned on her heels, and yelled down the aisle. 'You there! All of you! This is God's work you're about to see!' 'Shut up,' said the Angel. 'She's going to kill us, because she doesn't want us human.'

The choir had forsaken the Requiem entirely now. Two of the tenors were sobbing, and one of the altos had lost control of her bladder, and was splashing loudly on the marble steps. 'Don't look away!' Theresa told them. 'You have to remember this forever.' 'That won't save you,' Sophus said. Her wrists were beginning to glow. Some withering blast was undoubtedly simmering there. 'Will you ... hold my hand?' Pidgin asked, tentatively reaching out for Theresa.

She smiled sweetly, and slipped her hand into his. Then—though they knew they could not escape the coming fire—they began to back away from its source, like a married couple running their ceremony in reverse. Behind them, the witnesses were sloping off. The conductor had taken refuge behind the pulpit, the basses had fled, every one; one of the sobbing tenors was digging for a handkerchief while the sopranos pushed past him to make their getaway. The Angel raised her murderous hands. 'It was fun while it lasted,' Pidgin murmured to Theresa, turning his eyes upon her so as not to see the blast when it came.

It didn't come. They retreated another step, and another, and still it didn't come. They both dared glance back towards the Angel, and found to their astonishment that Uncle Raymond had appeared from somewhere, and had thrown himself between them and the Angel's ire. He had clearly suffered in paradise. His cloth-of-gold raiment hung in tatters. His flesh was bloodied and bruised where he'd been repeatedly struck. But he had the strength of an unforgiven man. 'They're innocent!' he hollered. 'Like little children!'

Furious at this interference, Sophus Demdarita unleashed an incoherent yell, and with it the fire she'd intended for Pidgin and Theresa. It struck poor Pocock in his lawless groin—whether by chance or felicity nobody would ever know—and there began its devouring work. Raymond threw back his head and let out a sob that was in part agony and in part thankfulness, then, before the Angel could detach herself, reached up and drove his fingers deep into her eyes.

Angels are beyond physical suffering; it is one of their tragedies. But Raymond's fingers, turning to excrement in that very moment, found their way into Sophus Demdarita's cranium. Blinded by shit, the divine blaze staggered away from her victim, and met a wave of firemen and police officers as they entered the church behind her, axes and hoses at the ready. She threw her arms above her head, and ascended on a beam of flickering power, removing herself from the earthly plane before her presence grazed undeserving human flesh, and began a new game of consequences.

The seed of rot she had sown in Raymond's flesh did not cease to spread on her passing. He was withering into shit, and nothing could stop the process. By the time Pidgin and Theresa reached him he was little more than a head in a spreading pool of excrement. But he seemed happy enough. 'Well, well...' he said to the pair, '...what a day it's been.' He coughed up a wormy turd. 'I wonder ... did I maybe dream it all?' 'No,' Theresa said, brushing a stray hair from his eye. 'No, you didn't dream it.' 'Will she come again?' Pidgin wanted to know. 'Very possibly,' Raymond replied. 'But the world's wide, and she'll have my shit in her eyes to keep her from seeing you clearly. No need to live in fear. I did enough of that for all three of us.' 'Did they not want you in Heaven?' Theresa asked him. 'I'm afraid not,' he said. 'But having seen it, I'm not much bothered. One thing though...' His face was dissolving now, his eyes snaking away into his sockets. 'Yes?' said Pidgin. 'A kiss?' Theresa leaned down and laid her lips on his. The firemen and officers looked away in disgust. 'And you, my pet?' Pocock said to Pidgin. He was just a mouth now, puckered up on a pool of shit. Pidgin hesitated. 'I'm not your pet,' he said. The mouth had no time to apologize. Before it could form another syllable, it was unmade. 'I don't regret not having kissed him,' Pidgin remarked to Theresa as they wandered down the hill an hour or so later. 'You can be cold, parrot,' Theresa replied. Then, after a moment, she said: 'I wonder what the choristers will say, when they speak of this?' 'Oh, they'll invent explanations,' Pidgin replied. 'The truth won't come out.' 'Unless we tell it.' Theresa said. 'No,' Pidgin replied. 'We must keep it to ourselves.' 'Why?' 'Theresa, my love, isn't it obvious? We're human now. That means there's things we should avoid.' 'Angels?' 'Yes.' 'Excrement.' 'Yes.'

'And—?'

'The truth.'

'Ah,' said Theresa. 'The Truth.' She laughed lightly. 'From now, let's ban it from all conversation. Agreed?' 'Agreed,' he said, laying a little peck upon her scaly cheek. 'Shall I begin? Theresa said. 'By all means.'

'I loathe you, love. And the thought of making children with you disgusts me.' Pidgin brushed the swelling mound at the front of his trousers. 'And this,' he said, 'is a liquorice stick. And I can think of no fouler time to use it than now.'

So saying, they embraced with no little passion, and like countless couples wandering the city tonight, started in search of a place to entwine their limbs, telling fond lies to one another as they went.

An End to All Things

by Brian Keene

TODAY, LIKE EVERY other day, I got up and made some coffee. While it brewed, I changed from my bedroom slippers to my shoes. When the coffee was finished, I poured a mug, carried it outside, and walked down to the river. I made sure the belt on my bathrobe was cinched up tight, so it didn't drag in the goose shit that's all over the yard. But even with the belt tightened up, my robe hung loose. Probably from all the weight I've lost.

I stood there at the water's edge and waited for the world to end.

This morning I wished for global warming. That seems appropriate, given the weather. Seventy degrees in central Pennsylvania a few days before Christmas? If that's not a sign that global warming is a real thing, then I don't know what is. But the problem with global warming is that it's not fast enough. It's a creeping death. I needed something quick. I want the world to end today, not decades from now.

So I waited, steam rising from my mug, bathrobe blowing in the wind, and just like always, the world didn't end.

They say that magic is nothing more than physics—the art of bending the world around you to your will. If that is true, then I'm a terrible magician.

Far out across the water, a goose reared up, flapping its wings and chasing another. The other geese squawked in response, their angry honks echoing across the yard. Until we bought this house, I always assumed that geese flew south for the winter. And who knows? Maybe they still do. Maybe these particular geese just decided "Fuck it. You know what? It's seventy degrees here. Why bother flying any further south?"

Maybe the geese know something I don't. Maybe their magic is stronger.

I watched the river flow past, watched the rising sun reflect across the waves and eddies. I watched the windmills on the far shore, turning sluggishly, supplying electricity for Lancaster County. I watched a bass boat, far off in the distance, and the lone fisherman standing up inside of it. Eventually, once my coffee was finished, I turned around, walked back across the yard, and came inside.

It was only now, while writing this, that I realized something. While I was down at the river this morning, I managed not to look at that spot near the dock. That doesn't always happen. But today, it did.

I count that as a little victory.

Today, like every other day, I repeated my morning ritual: coffee, shoes, and then the riverbank. It is one day closer to Christmas and even warmer than it was yesterday. Global warming continues to disappoint me, so I wished for something else.

This morning, I choose the zombie apocalypse. Not the most realistic end of the world scenario, I know, but there was a show on television last night about zombies. I've never been much of a horror fan, but I watched the show all the same. I watched it the same way I watch all the other programs—because it's something to do while I wait. The people on the show had a lot of lines about how much it sucked to be them, and how their world was ending, and how unfair that was. I envied them. They have everything that I want.

No, zombies might not be the most realistic way for the world to end, but I wished for them anyway, because nothing else seems to work.

When I was done, I turned around to head back to the house.

But today...today I slipped up. Today, as I turned, I looked at that spot near the dock.

And there was Braylon—there was my little boy—drowning again.

Today, I wished for an asteroid strike. Nothing fancy, mind you. Just a giant chunk of space rock—something the size of Texas, maybe—hurtling out of the sky and smashing into Central Pennsylvania with enough impact to vaporize this fucking river and pummel the house into dust. But just like global warming and zombies, space let me down. I stood there a while, watching the sky, but the only thing I saw were airplanes, having departed from Harrisburg or Baltimore-Washington, carrying people somewhere else. I want to go somewhere else, too, but no airplane is going to take me there. I want to go wherever Braylon and Caroline are, but there are no direct flights. Train, buses, and airplanes don't go there, unless they crash. And even then, I might get unlucky and walk away.

There's only one other way to get there, and I am still too afraid to follow.

I kept staring up at the clouds, watching the airplanes. A new one seemed to cross the sky every five minutes or so. But there were no asteroids. No comets. No peace for me. I stared so long that I got a kink in my neck.

When I finally looked down again, there was Braylon, still wearing the same sweat pants ("comfy pants" were what he always called them) and the same Minecraft t-shirt he'd been wearing the last time I saw him there, and still clutching that orange butterfly net Caroline had bought him. Still pointing at the minnows clustered around the dock. I balled my hands into fists and closed my eyes, but that didn't stop me from hearing him.

Look, Dad! See all the baby fish? I bet I can catch some of them.

The first time he'd said that to me, as he'd crouched on the edge of the dock, dipping his net into the river, I'd opened my mouth to tell him to be careful. This time, when I opened my mouth, all that came out was a deep moan. My anguish almost drowned out the surprised—not frightened, but surprised—little yelp he made as he fell over the side; the yelp that was cut short a second later when his head hit the concrete edge.

I knew I'd see his blood there, slowly spreading in the water again, so I waited until I turned around before I opened my eyes.

I wept the whole way back to the house. My robe came unfastened and the belt hung down into the goose shit, but I didn't notice until later. Distraught, I collapsed onto the couch and cried myself back to sleep. It took a long time to accomplish that, but that was okay. The couch cushions still held my imprint from the night before.

I haven't slept in the bed—or even spent more than five minutes in the bedroom—since Caroline killed herself in it. All of her clothes, her shoes, her make-up and skin care products, and those little scented candles that she used to like, and everything else, is still in there. My clothes are in a laundry basket sitting on the floor in the living room. That's where they stay, except when I'm wearing them or washing them.

And Braylon's room?

I've been in there only once since he drowned. The day after it happened. Two days before the funeral. Three days before Caroline went to search for him, leaving me behind and alone in this place.

I haven't been back inside his room since, but I can picture it clearly. If I opened the door, I know what I would find inside, and exactly where everything would be. His bed would be rumpled and unmade, the circus animal patterned sheets and pillowcase still smelling like him. The floor would be covered with different action figures: Marvel and DC superheroes, Ben 10, Imaginext, Ninja Turtles, and Star Wars galore. The train table, left behind long after Braylon sold off his Thomas the Tank Engine toys at our yard sale because "they were for little kids and he was eight now" will still be covered with Legos, including the half-finished house we'd been building together. A house that will never be finished. A house that is incomplete. A house that is haunted.

Just like this house.

Today I wished for a terrorist attack.

Today it was raining, so I stayed inside and wished the world would flood and the river would rise and the water would wash it all away—me and the house and the bedroom and Braylon's room and all the stuff and all the ghosts.

Today I wished for a pandemic. Not something like the flu, which takes a long time to spread effectively. No, I wished for something like Ebola on crack. Something that would spread like wildfire, engulfing the world. Engulfing me

I took my temperature when I came inside, but it was normal.

I said before that I don't watch a lot of horror movies. That's because most of them are stupid. Take ghost movies, for example. The house is haunted and terrible things are happening, but do the people in those movies ever do the logical thing and just fucking leave? No. They stay in the house. They refuse to move.

I never understood that until after Braylon and Caroline were gone. After they were buried, and everyone had offered their condolences, and I was here, alone. After the house had been professionally cleaned and the police had finished their investigation and all of Caroline's blood had been scrubbed off the walls and the carpet. And even then, sitting here on that first night, biting through my bottom lip so I wouldn't scream, wondering what to do with the rest of my life, wondering how to even have a rest of my life, I still didn't understand why the people in those movies never moved. It wasn't until I thought about selling the house and found out exactly how little chance of that I had in this economy, and how much I still owed the bank, that I began to understand. It wasn't until a friend, one of the last friends I spoke to before everyone stopped coming around, told me I should get away for a while, take a vacation or buy an RV and just go, somewhere far away from here and start over—that those movies started to make sense to me. It wasn't until I started seeing Braylon over and over again down by the river, and hearing his laughter—and hearing the sound his head made as it struck the dock—that I understood completely. It wasn't until I started sleeping on the couch, waking up every morning disheveled and feeling hopeless and aching from my knees up to my neck while the echo of that gunshot rang in my head again and again and again, that I empathized with the people in those films.

It's not that those people don't want to leave the haunted house. It's that they can't.

And neither can I.

Today I went down to the river and I wished for suicide by cop. Or, to be more accurate, I wished that I could figure out a way to make suicide by cop happen. I was never a sportsman, so it's not like I have a lot of guns in the house. The only one we had was the .45 that Caroline used, and that's sitting in an evidence room at the State Police barracks. They said I could pick it up when the investigation was done, but I haven't bothered. If I did, I'd have to go down there and listen to them tell me how sorry they all were, and if I wanted that, I'd still have friends.

Even if I had a gun, I don't know who I'd shoot. I'm not mad enough at anybody to go on a shooting spree. I mean, I'm mad at the world. I'm mad at the universe. I want it all to end. But I don't hold anything against the other people still here. It would be one thing if a comet or an earthquake killed them all, but I don't have the courage to kill myself, let alone anyone else.

I could jump off a building, but knowing my luck, I'd end up paralyzed and stuck here, haunted day in and day out. I could take pills, but I don't know what to take, and again, there's no guarantee that an overdose would do the trick. I tried to look it up online, but it's not as easy to find that kind of information as they make it look on television.

Today is Christmas Eve. A year ago today Braylon and Caroline were here. We spent the day together. We let Braylon open one present before going to bed, with the promise that he could open all of the others—along with all the ones Santa Claus would bring—the next morning. He was still seven then, and still believed in Santa Claus. Four months later he asked me for the truth and I asked him what he thought, and he wasn't sure.

He's gone now. He's gone and I never got to find out if he'd figured it out or not.

This morning, I wished that the super-volcano beneath Yellowstone would explode, covering the United States in molten ash, and making the sky as grey as I feel.

The geese are finally gone. Headed south, I suppose, even though the temperatures are still in the low Seventies. It's funny. I kind of miss seeing them, and hearing them. Now it's just me, again. Me and the memories of my wife and son.

Their ghosts are getting louder.

Today, is Christmas, but it's really just like every other day. I got up and made some coffee. While it brewed, I changed from my bedroom slippers to my shoes. When the coffee was finished, I poured a mug, carried it outside, and walked down to the river. My bathrobe hangs looser than ever.

I'm sitting here at the water's edge and waiting for the world to end.

This morning I wished for Three Mile Island to go into meltdown. It's only six miles up the river. But just like always, it didn't happen.

It's even warmer today than it was yesterday. Much too warm for Christmas in Pennsylvania. The perfect weather for swimming.

I'm sitting here writing this, and looking over at the spot where Braylon fell in, and I know his blood isn't there anymore, splashed all over the corner of the dock, but I see it anyway. I see the ghost.

An End to All Things

I'm going to finish this, and then I'm going to sit down on the edge of the dock, and put my feet in the water for a while. And who knows? As warm as it is, maybe I'll go swimming. I don't have the balls to kill myself, but maybe I can just swim until I'm tired. God knows it shouldn't take too long. I'm always tired these days.

I wonder if I'll see his ghost down there, under the water? I wonder if they'll be waiting for me, in wherever it is we go after this world ends?

CEMETERY DANCE

BY RICHARD CHIZMAR

ELLIOTT FOSSE, AGE thirty-three, small-town accountant. Waiting alone. Dead of winter. After midnight. The deserted gravel parking lot outside of Winchester County Cemetery.

Elliott stared out the truck window at the frozen darkness. His thoughts raced back to the handwritten note in his pants pocket. He reached down and squeezed the denim. The pants were new—bought for work not a week ago and still stiff to the touch—but Elliott could feel the reassuring crinkle of paper inside the pocket.

While the woman on the radio droned on about a snow warning for the entire eastern sector of the state, storm winds rumbled outside, buffeting the truck. Elliott's breath escaped in visible puffs and, despite the lack of heat in the truck, he wiped beads of moisture from his face. With the same hand, he snatched a clear pint bottle from the top of the dash and guzzled, tilting it upward long after it ran dry. He tossed the bottle on the seat next to him—where it clinked against two others—and reached for the door handle.

The wind grabbed him, lashing at his exposed face, and immediately the sweat on his cheeks frosted over. He quickly pulled the flashlight from his pocket and straightened his jacket collar, shielding his neck. The night sky was starless, enveloping the cemetery like a huge, black circus tent. His bare hands shook uncontrollably, the flashlight beam fluttering over the hard ground. Somewhere, almost muffled by the whine of the wind, he heard a distant clanking—a dull sound echoing across the grounds. He hesitated, tried to recognize the source, but failed.

Snow coming soon, he thought, gazing upward.

He touched a hand to the lopsided weight in his coat pocket and slowly climbed the cracked steps leading to the monument gate. During visiting hours, the gate marked the cemetery's main entrance and was always guarded by a groundskeeper, a short, roundish fellow with a bright red beard. But, at one in the morning, the grounds were long closed and abandoned.

Elliott's legs ached with every step. The liquor in his system was no match for the strength of the storm. His eyes and ears stung from the frigid blasts of wind. He longed to rest, but the contents of the note in his pocket pushed him onward. As he reached the last step, he was greeted by a rusty, fist-sized padlock banging loudly against the twin gates. It sounded like a bell tolling, warning the countryside of some unseen danger.

He rested for a moment, supporting himself against the gate, grimacing from the sudden shock of cold steel. He rubbed his hands together, then walked toward a narrow opening, partly concealed by a clump of scrubby thorn bushes, where the fence nearly connected with the gate's left corner. Easing his body through the space, Elliott felt the familiar tingle of excitement return. He had been here many times before … many times.

But tonight was different.

Creeping among the faded white headstones, Elliott noticed for the first time that their placement looked rather peculiar, as if they'd been dropped from the sky in some predetermined pattern. From above, he ruminated, the grounds must look like an overcrowded housing development.

Glancing at the sky again, thinking: Big snow on the way, and soon. He moved slower now, still confident, but careful not to pass the gravestone.

He had been there before, so many times, but he remembered the first time most vividly—fifteen years ago, during the day.

Everyone had been there. A grim Elliott standing far behind Kassie's parents, hidden among the mourning crowd. Her father, standing proudly, a strong hand on each son's shoulder. The mother, clad in customary black, standing next to him, choking back the tears.

Immediately following the service, the crowd had left the cemetery to gather at her parent's home, but Elliott had stayed. He had waited in the upper oak grove, hidden among the trees. When the workers had finished the burial, he had crept down the hill and sat, talking with his love on the fresh grave. And it had been magical, the first time Kassie really talked to him, shared herself with him. He'd felt her inside him that day and known that it had been right—her death, his killing, a blessing.

High above the cemetery, a rotten tree limb snapped, crashed to the ground below. Elliott's memory of Kassie's funeral vanished. He stood motionless, watching the bare trees shake and sway in the wind, dead branches scraping and rattling against each other. A hazy vision of dancing skeletons and demons surfaced in his mind. It's called the cemetery dance, the demons announced, glistening worms squirming from their rotten, toothless mouths. Come dance with us, Elliott, they invited, waving long, bony fingers. Come. And he wanted to go. He wanted to join them. They sounded so inviting. Come dance the cemetery dance …

He shook the thoughts away—too much liquor; that's all it was—and walked into a narrow gully, dragging his feet through the thin blanket of fallen leaves. He recognized the familiar row of stone markers ahead and slowed his pace. Finally, he stopped, steadied the bright beam on the largest slab.

The marker was clean and freshly cared for, the frozen grass around it still neatly trimmed. There were two bundles of cut flowers leaning against it. Elliott recognized the fresh bundle he'd left just yesterday, during his lunch break. He crept closer, bending to his knees. Tossing the flashlight aside, he eased next to the white granite stone, touching the deep grooves of the inscription, slowly caressing each letter, stopping at her name.

"Kassie," he whispered, the word swept away with the wind. "I found it, love." He dug deep in his front pocket, pulled out a crumpled scrap of lined white paper. "I couldn't believe you came to me again after all these years. But I found the note on my pillow where you left it."

Sudden tears streamed down his face. "I always believed you'd forgive me. I truly did. You know I had to do it ... it was the only way. You wouldn't even look at me back then," he pleaded. "I tried to make you notice me, but you wouldn't. So I had to."

The cemetery came to life around him, breathing for the dead. The wind gained strength, plastering leaves against the tree trunks and the taller headstones. Elliott gripped the paper tightly in his palm, protecting it from the night's constant pull.

"I'm coming now, love." He laughed with nervous relief. "We can be together, forever." He pulled his hand from his coat pocket and looked skyward. Snow coming, now. Anytime. A sudden gust of wind sent another branch crashing to the ground where it shattered into hundreds of jagged splinters.

Two gravestones away from it, Elliott collapsed hard to the earth, fingers curled around the pistol's rubber handgrip, locked there now. The single gunshot echoed across the cemetery until the storm swallowed it. Bits of glistening brain tissue sprayed the air, and mixed with the wooden splinters, showering the corpse. His mangled head lolled to the side, spilling more shiny gray matter onto the grassy knoll.

For just one moment, an ivory sliver of moonbeam slipped through the darkness, quickly disappeared. As the crumpled scrap of paper—scrawled in Elliott's own handwriting—was lifted into the wind's possession, the towering trees, once again, found their dancing partners. And it began to snow.

DRAWN TO THE FLAME

BY KEVIN QUIGLEY

THE SKULL, PERCHED on the top of a pointed stick and looking down at the boys with age-encrusted sockets, didn't look like it was human.

"What is that?" Johnny asked Chip, pointing up with fear.

"Probably a gorilla or something," Chip said, shrugging it off. Johnny felt a little better. Chip knew a lot of stuff—he was ten.

"I don't know, Chip," Bobby said, still staring up at the big thing. "There were pictures of gorilla skulls in our science books last year, and that don't look like the ones I saw."

Johnny looked over at Chip, who at first looked kind of angry, then smiled a little and explained, "It's just a skull anyway. It won't hurt you, right?"

Bobby took his eyes away and looked at Chip. "Yeah, I guess."

Chip said, "Good, now let's go. I don't want to stand in line for hours."

The boys walked away from the skull, heading toward the entrance. Johnny got a little thrill inside that was half fear, half excitement when he passed under the sign that said SCARY WORLD. This was gonna be great.

Oh boy, the carnival! Sweet, sugary cotton candy, the aroma floating through the air like a cloud. The sounds of the barkers calling out, "One dolla!" and "Fun, fun, fun!" and "Three tries, win a prize!" Tall, lumbering creatures with fearsome heads you knew were just men on stilts inside but still they scared you. Hot dogs and hamburgers, roasted peanuts, and fried dough all begging to be bought and eaten. Johnny loved carnivals. All the people—even grownups—coming to be thrilled or scared or made happy. The carnival was a magical place. He couldn't really say that type of thing to Chip or even Bobby, but he felt it in his heart. A magical place, and he felt magical inside of it.

They had all agreed, though, that the best part of the carnival was always the spook house. In the dark, scared out of your wits, pretending that it was no big deal when you came back into the light. One time, at the county fair in Scattersborough, Johnny and Bobby rode the House of Evil together. By the time the giant Dracula face lit up and seemed to jump at them, Bobby started screaming. When they got out, he tried to tell Johnny he was just doing it to scare him, but no way did Johnny believe that. He told Chip and they teased Bobby about it for months.

Then, the most amazing thing happened. They were all watching TV at Chip's house when they saw a commercial for something called Scary World. Until then, they'd been horsing around, play wrestling and laughing so hard that it sometimes hurt, but when the commercial came on, they all stopped.

"Do you like to be scared?" a deep, grating voice asked them through the TV. They all looked up. The TV showed a guy dressed up like a werewolf coming toward them. Johnny's eyes went wide. Yes, definitely, he liked to be scared.

"Then come to Scary World!" Now there was a spooky clown with blood running down his face dancing in slow motion. Johnny's heart leapt while his stomach clenched in fear.

"Games! Rides! Five new spook houses!" Five, did the voice say? Five spook houses?

"Open every night in October! Come one, come all!" At that moment, they all decided to be three of the ones that just had to go.

"No way in hell," said Chip's Mom. Johnny's Mom and Bobby's Mom had similar opinions. "You're too young," they said. "It's too scary."

Leave it to Chip to come up with a plan. The second Saturday in the month, Chip and Johnny told their Moms they were staying over Bobby's. Bobby told his Mom he was sleeping over at Chip's. They all met up at the cross-city bus stop near the edge of town, giggling and not believing they actually got away with it.

Now, here they were: in the middle of Scary World, all by themselves. Johnny had never been this happy.

"Hello, hello, hello boys!" a tall man in a tall hat said to them, bending down and grinning a huge, toothy grin. Johnny and Bobby recoiled a bit, but Chip just laughed.

"Who are you?" Chip asked, smiling.

The man stood up at full height.

"I am one Etienne LaRue,
master of Scary World, how about you?"

They all laughed a little, but Johnny felt some fear, too. This guy didn't seem right.

"I'm Chip," Chip said, "And this is Bobby and Johnny."

Mr. LaRue put his hands on hips and grinned even wider. "Chip, Bobby, and Johnny, young lads! Are you ready for all of the scares to be had?"

Chip laughed out loud this time. Johnny smiled too, but he felt a little nervous. Weren't they never supposed to talk to strangers?

"Come one, come three, I'll show you 'round
there's many thrills here to be found!
If getting spooked is your aim
why don't you try Drawn to the Flame?"

"Drawn to the Flame?" Johnny asked. "Is that a game?"

LaRue looked down at Johnny as if he were a bug. He bent down and showed his teeth again, but this time Johnny didn't think he was smiling.

"Drawn to the Flame is not a game
for it's a thrill upon that hill."

LaRue pointed, and for a second Johnny could only look at the man's trembling, outstretched finger. It was huge, longer than it should have been, ending in a yellowed, cracked fingernail. Johnny thought back to the skull near the entrance gate. It really hadn't been human, had it? If it hadn't, what about Mr. LaRue? Real fear began to creep into Johnny's belly, but before he could say or do anything, Chip hit him in the shoulder and Johnny turned.

There it was, on a far hill past all the other attractions. It was a spook house, not brightly lit like all the others, and it looked like it was falling apart.

"That's a spook house?" Bobby asked, and Johnny could hear the fear in his voice.

"It's the spookiest of them all," LaRue began,
"As you soon shall see!
Its thrills and chills are all first-rate
and guaranteed by me!"

Johnny was already spooked, though. Looking at the house far away on that hill made him feel more than scared. It made him feel bad all over.

"I don't..." he began, but then Chip leaned over and whispered in his ear, "You chicken?"

"No," Johnny said, and he swallowed, trying to make some of that bad feeling go away. When LaRue began to walk toward Drawn to the Flame, Chip followed him. Reluctantly, Johnny caught up to Chip, Bobby hanging back but still coming.

"Johnny?" Bobby asked suddenly, making Johnny jump up a little. "This is okay, right?"

Johnny looked up past the lights, past the other rides, up onto the hill where the creepy, creaky black house stood. It was the spookiest of them all, all right.

"Yeah, it's okay," he said, but when he tried to smile, he couldn't. He was too afraid.

"Where are all the lights?" Bobby whispered to Johnny in a trembling voice. Johnny jumped up a little, startled by the sudden noise. The path they were walking on wasn't lit, and Johnny turned back to look at the lights of Scary World. They seemed far away.

"I don't know," Johnny whispered back, feeling almost as scared as Bobby sounded. He was about to say something again when Mr. LaRue interrupted.

"Why are there no lights, you ask?" his voice boomed out over the long expanse of flat, shadowy earth between the park and the hill,

> "Can't see what's before your eyes?
> Why, if lights shone out everywhere
> it would ruin the big surprise!"

Johnny nodded, but Mr. LaRue's rhymes were getting creepy. Especially in the dark, with only the moon shining up above. In this hazy time of night, it was hard to see the tall man's face.

"Would you guys shut up?" Chip spat, sounding angry. Johnny knew better. Underneath the anger in Chip's voice, Johnny heard fear, and if Chip was afraid...

"Well, here we are, my fine young boys, tread gently on the stair! Enter the door, step inside, get ready for a scare!"

They were there, at the small set of steps that led to the porch of the house. A giant, rickety door stood slightly ajar at their end of the porch. Painted above the doorway, the words DRAWN TO THE FLAME stood out in yellow contrast to the drab, creepy outer wall. Something squishy and crawly moved around in Johnny's stomach. All at once, he felt like he was going to puke. LaRue scurried up the stairs, throwing open the door and grinning fiercely.

"Unless you're scared, then come on in, there's terror to be had within!" he cackled. Chip clambered up the stairs slowly, hesitating at the open door. He looked back at Johnny with doubt in his eyes.

"Go on," LaRue said, still grinning but letting it drop a little, "Go on, step through the door. Tell me, boy, what are you waiting for?"

Chip turned away from Johnny, seemed to breathe in deeply, and stepped up and over the doorjamb. He was swallowed in blackness immediately.

Go, now! Johnny's mind commanded, and he rushed up the steps after his friend, plunging through the door and bumping into Chip before his mind could counter: I meant the other way! Bobby, calling out "Wait, you guys!" followed last, colliding with the other two, cramped in the small, dark entry way to the house.

"Wait," Chip said, his voice coming vaguely from the left of Johnny, "Didn't he want tickets?"

Then, the door slammed behind them, immersing them in darkness. All three cried out, and the haunting, disembodied voice of Mr. LaRue called to them from outside:

"Now you're trapped, you stupid boys
it's all worked out as planned!"

Johnny realized for the first time that he very small, very scared, and his parents had no idea where he was.

"You're young and fresh, and caught like mice
and feeding time is now at hand."

"What?" gasped Bobby, clutching onto Johnny. "Is this part of the spook house?"

"Shhh!" Chip hissed. Bobby fell silent, and now Johnny could hear something in the high, unseen ceilings of the house. It sounded like … something rustling, like those Oriental hand-fans his Mom liked to use in the summer. A delicate sound, but somehow sinister.

Like the fans: flap, flap, flap, all in darkness.

"Let's get out of here," Chip said, his voice cracking. They started walking forward, Johnny feeling his way along the pitch black corridor. His crawly, nervous stomach was now doing somersaults and his brain was screaming out Run! Run! He wanted to answer Bobby. No, this wasn't part of the spook house. This is for real.

Just then, a light came on in a far corner, accompanied by a heavy slamming sound. Suddenly, they could see where they were standing: a charred wreck of a former hallway with flame-scarred floors and peeling, burnt wallpaper hanging in tatters all around them. The light, coming from the floor, was situated at the end of the hall in a kitty-corner, pointed up at the ceiling.

Another light came on with the same bang, this one much closer to them, also pointed up at the ceiling. All was quiet but for the steady flap, flap, flap rustling coming from above.

What is it? one side of his mind questioned in a panicky, terrified voice.

Run! the other side commanded in a strange tone very similar to the first.

His better judgement almost won out: he almost pushed the other two ahead, saying Go! Hurry! But he was eleven, and his curiosity got the better of him.

He looked up. They all looked up.

That was when the moths attacked.

Johnny screamed, his eyes opening wide, as he watched the small flying insects descend. There were hundreds, no, thousands of them, battering the air with their soft, paper-thin wings. In droves they came down from the high ceiling, the beating of their million wings drowned out only by the sound of his friends' screams. The only distinct words came from his left, from Chip, screaming at them to run, you guys, run!

For a moment, Johnny couldn't. Couldn't tear his staring, frightened eyes from the gigantic flapping gray mass above him. Couldn't stop looking up, waiting for them to reach him, waiting to see what would happen...

Then Chip was yanking on the sleeve of his shirt, and he turned away from the moths. Chip and Bobby's faces were white, almost sickly in this artificial light. They both looked terrified.

"The door!" Chip screamed, and a moth flew into the side of his face. Chip slapped at it, squashing it against his skin. "Oh, gross!" Bobby said, and for a second, Johnny could only look at his friend, unable to take his eyes off the icky, brown-red splotch left on his cheek. Then, more moths came, pounding at him like hundreds of small missiles. Johnny lowered his head and put his arms over it to shield himself, screamed and began running back toward the door.

More lights came on, dotting the hallway like the running lights at a movie theater, only brighter. Moths poured down upon him, slamming into his body and bounding off. The feeling like he was going to puke was even stronger now. Tilting his head up a little, Johnny could see the door up ahead, the one they had stepped through only a few short minutes before. He reached out one small hand and moths tried to light on it, flapping away when they realized his hand was a moving target.

Praying that it wasn't locked, Johnny grabbed out at the doorknob, turning.

It was locked.

"Oh shit!" he cried out, and Chip collided with him. Through his old Sharks T-shirt, Johnny could feel about a dozen moth-bodies crunching in between his back and Chip's stomach. Now, he finally did throw up, feeling his lunch of hot dogs and beans flow freely from his stomach and land in a steaming heap on the floor near the door. Johnny suddenly felt horribly weak.

"The ... stairs, John," he heard Chip say from behind him. It sounded like Chip was having trouble keeping lunch down, too. "Up there!" Johnny glanced around and saw them—rotted, burned stairs leading up into darkness. A spooky black room scattered with decrepit furniture stood between he and the stairs, but it didn't look all that large to Johnny and he hoped against hope that there wasn't anything hiding in there.

"I don't want to go up there!" Bobby wailed. Johnny turned and saw Bobby slapping away teeming swarms of moths. "It's dark up there!"

Chip yelled back, "Right, they won't follow us! They only come when there's light!"

Drawn to the flame, Johnny thought, oh God we shoulda known.

Johnny lurched ahead, careful to step over his own puke, and made his way to the stairwell. The stairs—thirty or so in all—didn't look very safe, like they would collapse if even one of them climbed up, let alone three.

"Go, Johnny!" Chip screamed from behind.

"What if they fall?" Johnny screamed back.

"They won't fall!" Chip said, pushing Johnny roughly upward. "Go!"

Gulping, Johnny grabbed the banister, feeling some of the char giving way under his hand. He pushed up with his foot, leaping up two stairs at a time, only looking up. They're gonna break he thought, fear pounding his heart faster and faster, oh God, they're gonna break.

Then, he was at the top of the stairs, standing in a new hall-way that was thankfully unlit. He turned back and looked down at his friends. Chip pounded up the blackened stairs, taking them like Johnny had, two at a time. Bobby brought up the rear, clutching onto the banister with both hands and looking down, coming up slowly.

Chip made it to the top, leaping from the stairs and putting his arms out so he didn't bang into the wall on the other side. Johnny looked down, sweat standing out on his face.

"Come on, Bobby!" he whisper-screamed. He'd seen enough cartoons to know that if you yelled real loud in some places, everything came crashing down.

"It's gonna break," he heard Bobby whine from halfway up, and he was about to say No it ain't, when he heard something crack.

"That's the railing," Chip whispered at him, shocked. "Oh my God, the railing's gonna break off!"

"Let go of the railing, Bobby!" Johnny called down. Bobby turned to face his friends, letting go of the railing. "Why?" he called up.

Just then, the railing creaked more, and whatever nails had held the burnt length of wood in place gave way. The nails screeched, and the railing tilted outward, holding for a second, then breaking off and crashing to the floor below.

"Bobby!" Johnny screamed. Too late to play it safe now. Bobby was staring down at the floor where the railing had landed. "Bobby!" he screamed again, louder. "Run, now!"

Another creak echoed in the darkness. From the lit hallway came the ever-present sounds of the kamikaze moths flapping their wings.

Bobby took one nervous step upward, placing a delicate foot on the stair above the one he was standing on. He hitched in a breath, but Johnny looked closer at Bobby's down-turned face and guessed it might have been a sob. It looked like Bobby was crying.

Oh, jeez, Johnny thought, and the stairs creaked again, louder this time. Instead of forcing Bobby up faster, the noise seemed to have frozen him in place.

"Hurry!" Chip yelled, and Bobby looked up.

"I can't," Bobby moaned, and the loudest creak yet bounced off the walls of the small, furniture-strewn room.

"Oh little boys, fresh little boys!" a voice—LaRue's—boomed, seeming to come from everywhere. It had a tinny sound like the loudspeakers at school, Johnny thought, cringing.

> *"You think you've won the race?*
> *My little pets are hungry*
> *and all they've got's a taste!"*

LaRue's rhyme ended in a long, sinister cackle, accompanied by the same loud slamming sound they'd heard in the bottom hallway. Almost immediately, a huge, humming fluorescent popped on just above the doorway where Johnny and Chip now stood.

"Oh God," Johnny said, his brain a Tilt-a-Whirl of fear. Without thinking, he leapt from the doorway, pounding down the stairs. Bobby, who looked more scared than ever, shrieked girlishly when Johnny grabbed him by the wrist and yanked him upward. A furtive glance behind him showed Johnny what he already knew: some of the moths were leaving the hallway and swarming toward the new light source at the top of the dark, dark room. His blood thumping thickly in his veins, Johnny glanced back at the stairs, and tripped, falling on his belly, his head banging against one of the top stairs. Bobby, still continuing on Johnny's momentum, took the remaining stairs quickly. Johnny slowly got to his knees and palms, shaking his head. He could already feel a bump forming there. Carefully, he got to his feet, and took one step up.

The stairway let out one alarmingly loud creak, and Johnny's blood froze. He felt a tremor beneath him, and all of a sudden, the top of the stairs sunk downward. Johnny canted to the right, holding out his arms to maintain his balance. Ahead of him, his friends were yelling at him to run. Behind him, the sound of the horrible, oncoming moths got louder. Johnny didn't hear much of either. His eyes and mind were focused down to the floor below, where the creaking, cracking stairs were about to fall, carrying a small heap of boy with them.

Down I go, he thought, and then the first of the moths flew into him, slapping against the back of his neck and fluttering in his hair.

The reality of the moths awoke him from the dark fantasy of falling. He glanced up, saw the sloping steps detached from the doorway up there, and nearly panicked. I can't get there, he thought, and a moth flapped into his ear, creating a horrid, squelchy rustling noise that seemed to take over his brain.

Johnny screamed, pushing up on his higher leg and forcing his other leg to follow. One, two, three running steps, and right before he slammed his foot down on the first of the falling stairs, he pushed off and found himself flying.

For a second, everything else stopped. All the panic in his brain, all the moth-noise in his ear, all the acrid, vomity taste in his mouth went away, and he was airborne, he was free. The feeling ended abruptly as he landed in the doorway, crouching and rolling against the wall facing the opening. His knee connected with the broken-off jut of the top stair and he cried out.

Hurriedly, Johnny dug his finger in his ear, poking at the moth lodged in there, and killing it instantly. He scraped out the bloody remains, feeling queasy again, and wiped his finger on the leg of his jeans.

"Are you okay?" Bobby asked almost reverently, bending down and putting a hand on Johnny's shoulder.

"Fine," Johnny managed, his mind becoming full with the thought of the moths again. He opened his eyes and turned his head around. Here they came, teeming toward the light and the boys who sat under it. "Go, go!" he yelled, trying to stand. Putting pressure on the hurt knee caused his leg to buckle, and he would have fallen if Chip hadn't grabbed him and hoisted him into a standing position.

"Where to?" Chip asked, and Johnny squinted down the new corridor they stood in. A stray moth flickered into view and he batted it away from his field of vision. A series of doors dotted the hallway on both sides, and any of them looked as good as any other. A frozen moment passed, but then he remembered something his Dad had done a couple years ago, trying to pick out a vacation spot. Dad had spread out a map on the dining room table, closed his eyes, and plunked his index finger down. They ended up going to Disneyworld, so that seemed, to Johnny at least, a good method of picking things.

He closed his eyes, hearing the rush of the oncoming moths, and pointed. "There!" he said, and opened his eyes. Chip began moving—and moving Johnny, too—before Johnny even opened his eyes to know which one he picked. Bobby ran ahead and stopped at the door the second from the back on the left-hand side.

"Please don't be locked," Johnny heard Bobby moan, unable to see him clearly because his and Chip's shadows obscured Bobby in black. Chip rushed him along, and when they were in front of the door, Bobby turned the knob. The door was unlocked.

"Thank you God," Johnny said, moving his arm from around Chip's shoulders and following Bobby into the mine-dark room. Chip followed behind quickly and slammed the door behind them. Johnny heard the sickening sound of a dozen or so moths battering against the hard wood on the other side of the door.

"Now what?" Bobby asked.

"Now what what?" Johnny asked back, spread-eagled against the door in case the moths found some way to push their way in.

"What do we do now?"

"I don't know!" The panic was coming back. Johnny thought he had never wanted his mother more. How easy it would be to just cry now, just sit down in this dark room and curl up into a ball and just cry.

No! he thought. It's just a house, there's gotta be a way out!

"Maybe there's a door on the other side of the room!" Chip said in a scared, trembly voice. Johnny couldn't see anything, but he felt Chip getting ready to run.

"No, man, don't!" Johnny spat, putting his arm out to hold his friend in place. "We don't know what's in the room!"

A few seconds ticked by. Johnny's mind raced.

"We can't just stay here!" Chip shouted, breaking away from Johnny.

"No!" Johnny called out, hearing Bobby echo him close by. "Chip, stop!"

Johnny heard his footsteps beating against the floor, but didn't know which direction they were going. In this total blackness, sounds were funny. The running steps could be going anywhere, any direction.

Then, just as they had started, they just as quickly stopped. Johnny heard Chip mutter some sound—"Ooof!"—and there was a noise of somebody running into something.

He ran into the far wall, Johnny thought, now feeling cold pressed against the door. That's all. But he didn't believe it.

Almost immediately following the collision sound, Johnny heard another: the clear, definite sound of something heavy being slid on a track. Like the back porch door at home, he thought. But why...?

The sliding-door sound stopped, and very, very faintly, Johnny thought he could hear somebody breathing.

LaRue! Oh my God he's in here with us!

Then, another sliding-door sound, faster this time, and another, and another. Now, the light sound of breathing was heavier, as if someone—LaRue—were exerting himself.

"What's going on?" Bobby moaned. He had moved closer to Johnny and now he grabbed his arm. "Johnny, what's happening?"

Suddenly, in the center of the room, a light came on. Johnny shielded his now dilated eyes, then slowly opened them.

"Oh," he said in a very small voice. "Oh my God."

The sliding sounds really had been sliding glass doors, set in what looked like heavy metal frames, just like the one at home. There were four of them, crossing the length of the room on a door-track set into the wood of the floor. About a foot behind the glass, what looked like wall crisscrossed with planks of plywood had been constructed. Between the glass and the wood was Chip, illuminated by hanging ceiling-lights, lying on the ground.

"What...?" Bobby asked. Johnny ignored him.

"Chip, wake up!" he screamed. "He's got you trapped, you gotta wake up! You—"

Then, the mellifluous, taunting voice of Etienne LaRue filled the room, shocking Johnny's words out of him.

"So far from home, you came for chills
a little scare's what brought you here
But now, my boys, just watch and learn
this small experiment in fear."

At the words, Chip began to stir. Johnny's voice found him again and he called out to his friend. "Chip, get up, you've gotta get outta there!"

"What?" Chip asked from behind the glass, pulling himself to a sitting position and rubbing the front of his head. His voice was muffled, sounding far-off and unreal.

"Get out of there!" Johnny said, breaking from the door and running over to the glass. Then, for a second, the room was in darkness again. Johnny stopped, and the light came back on. He stood for a second between door and glass, and it happened again, faster this time. The lights flicked off, then on. Faster: off, on, off on, off on, off on.

Strobe lights? Johnny thought, thinking back to the ones his school used when the fifth graders did Pirates of Penzance last year. What...?

He looked up at the lights, trying to focus. A small trapdoor opened in the ceiling, in between two of the lights. A pair of swift hands came into view holding a large canvas bag. The hands let the bag drop, and it landed next to Chip with a floomph sound.

Then, Johnny realized. He saw.

From the bag, a lone moth twittered out. Soon, a second followed, then a third, then a dozen. Chip, who seemed to still be coming back to himself, stared at the bag in horror. More moths flew up and out toward the strobe lights. Chip leapt up from the floor and began to scream. Johnny ran up to the glass and put his palms on the cool surface of one of the doors, trying to move it either way. It was impossible; the doors were too heavy.

Another canvas bag dropped from the ceiling, and more moths swarmed out. In the flickering, disorienting light, the moths seemed to be jerking back and forth instead of flying. Chip ran back and forth, screaming, seeming to be pantomiming in quick-flash statue-poses. Johnny banged on the glass. "Let him out! Please let him out!"

The haunting, disembodied voice of LaRue spoke up.

"My pets are hungry, can't you see
it's really very funny
'cause when they're through with a Chip or two
they might make room for Johnny!"

Johnny screamed, pounding his fists against the glass. Another bag flooomphed down, and more moths burred out. The glass enclosure now teemed with moths, their brown-gray bodies flickering together madly in the off/on light. Johnny watched Chip scream again, and a moth flew into his mouth. Chip's scream abruptly ended, followed by a harsh gagging sound.

"No, no!" Johnny screamed, trying desperately to budge the doors, his hands squeaking across the glass surface. In upsetting, nightmarish slow motion, Chip fell to the floor, the strobes flickering over his body. He gagged again and the moth that had flown into his mouth came tumbling wetly out. In one of the swift bursts of blue-white light, Johnny saw a congregation of moths zoom toward Chip's face from the most recently opened bag.

Don't scream, Chip, Johnny thought, don't open your mouth!

But Chip did scream; he probably couldn't help it. He stood, throwing up his arms to shield his eyes, but his gaping, yelling mouth was left exposed. The moths zeroed in on their target, like a group of fighter planes in formation, and half a dozen moths slammed into Chip's mouth.

Again, Chip's screams stopped. His small hand pressed flat against the surface of the glass and his knees seemed to go weak. The upper half of his body stooped, and now he looked like Old Mrs. Engle who lived down the street, who was eighty-five and walked hunched over all the time. Without thinking, Johnny put his hand on his side of the glass, mirroring Chip's. Moths buzzed around his head like an angry gray-black cloud, shifting and moving like something large and solid. Chip's eyes bugged out, his other shaky hand going to his throat, clutching it.

He can't breathe, Johnny thought. Weakly, he banged on the glass with the fist not held up against Chip's. "Let him out," he gasped, but there was no strength in it.

Another small swarm of moths flew at Chip's face, and Johnny watched in horror as two of them lodged themselves up Chip's nostrils. Chip let go of the glass, staggering blindly to the center of the glass-and-wood enclosure. His other hand flew up to his throat now, but he didn't clutch with this one. He clawed.

"Oh God," Johnny said, putting his other palm flat against the glass. Chip dug his fingernails into his throat, drawing four tracks of instantly seeping red. He clawed again, this time with both hands, tearing his neck apart. Johnny watched his wide, staring eyes in the strobe, and they glowed like alien-eyes, moist and pleading.

Chip fell to the wooden floor with a thump, and that some-how scared Johnny most of all. A sack of potatoes made that type of thumping sound. What did that make Chip now?

He was aware of wetness on his cheeks, but he didn't care. Chip lay on the floor, convulsing. Some type of fluid was leaking out of his mouth, and that was something Johnny just couldn't watch. He felt sick to his stomach, and scared, and tired, and he just wanted to get out of there.

He turned from the glass cage. "Bobby!" he called. The lights still flickering showed no one at the door. Panicked again, Johnny called out his name again, louder: "BOBBY!"

The room fell silent. Now, he heard a low, pained sobbing off to one dark corner. He sprinted across the room that way, and saw Bobby there, huddled up into himself, crying.

"Bobby we have to go," Johnny said, wiping his own tears away.

"Did you see what they did?" Bobby asked, pointing at the cage.

For a second, memory tried to crowd Johnny's mind. Yes, of course he saw what they did. But he couldn't let that get to him now. He shook his head and said, "Yeah, but if we stay here, they'll do it to us, too."

Bobby was silent for a second, then his eyes closed tight and he started screaming.

I can't talk him out, Johnny thought, and grabbed his arm as he had on the stairs. Hoisting him up, Johnny caught a grip on Bobby's shirt and dragged him toward the door they'd come through.

Don't be locked, please don't be locked, his mind whis-pered. It was becoming a mantra, and for a moment, Johnny didn't know how he wanted his prayers answered. When he tried the knob, the door opened easily, and he shoved the still-screaming Bobby into the hallway. He took one look back in the room. Under the flickering lights, the moths were lighting on Chip's body, creating a moth-covered lump that might once have been a boy.

"Jeez, Chip," he said, then forced himself to turn and leave the room. The door he slammed behind him sounded like finality. Chip was dead. Jesus God, Chip was dead.

The hallway was dark. At some point during their time in the room, LaRue had shut off the light at the front of the hallway. Johnny looked nervously in that direction, then looked back to survey the mirror rows of doors just barely visible in the hallway.

"Come on," he said to Bobby, whose screams were trickling off now.

"Where?" Bobby wailed.

Johnny's mind tangled. He had no idea how to answer that question.

They stood in the dark, both trembling, unselfconsciously holding each other. Johnny had stopped crying, finally succeeding in his efforts to block Chip's death out of his head, if only for a short time. Bobby was in bad shape though. Johnny had heard on a show once that it was pretty easy to have a breakdown. They showed pictures of a girl in a hospital flipping out, screaming, crying and not being able to stop. What if that was happening with Bobby? What if he was having a break-down? How could you stop something like that?

We gotta get outta here, he thought feverishly. He tentatively let go of Bobby and stepped to the door behind his friend.

"Oh what fun!" the sudden, terrible voice of Etienne LaRue called out from his hidden speakers.

"Oh what fun is to be had
behind that door, there's nothing bad
open it, you might be free
or end up like Chip, try it and see!"

Johnny's hand hovered over the brass doorknob. He had to be honest with himself; he was not all that anxious to try it and see.

Wheeling around, he found another door and touched the surface. LaRue spoke up again, and this time his voice had a dangerous edge of dark hilarity. Like he was going to bust a gut laughing but for bad, bad reasons.

"Door number two,
just right for you
open it up and walk right through."

Johnny closed his eyes. Frustration as well as dread and panic had begun to fill him. Which door? Which way?
He touched another.

"Come on in
no need to fear
there's nothing bad
to be had in here."

Another.

"That's right, John
that's the door
go right through
see what's in store!"

"Shut up!" Johnny screamed upward. Tears flew from his eyes, but instead of indicating sadness or pain, they were tears of anger. "Shut the fuck up!"
He'd never said that word aloud before. It was powerful, liberating. Bobby, who had stopped crying when Johnny began to scream, just stared at him. Johnny grabbed him by the arm again (starting to feel like Bobby's keeper—which, in a way, he had become) and hauled him to the door at the very end of the hall.

"Ah, the door at the end," LaRue's voice called. Johnny ignored it.

"What a nice place to stop!"

"Shut up," Johnny mumbled, reaching out and grabbing the doorknob.

"But if I were you," LaRue went on. Johnny flung the door open. Inside, nothing but blackness.

"Come on," he told Bobby, stepping through the door, holding onto Bobby's arm.

"I'd watch out for the drop."

And suddenly he was falling, plunging down in darkness, and Bobby was beside him, also falling, and they were both screaming, and then they reached the bottom, hitting some solid ground, and Johnny kept screaming but horribly, terribly, Bobby had stopped.

Dark again, and pain. For a moment, Johnny could only lay there, still screaming, on whatever cold surface he had landed, stunned and scared and hurting. After his head had cleared from the horror of falling in the dark, his screams began to taper off and he was able to sit.

"Bobby?" he asked the room. Nothing. Then, with more panic in his voice, "Bobby?" Still nothing. Images filled his mind: Bobby landing on his head, blood oozing from his ears in lazy rivers, or maybe landing on his chest, sending shards of ribs through insides, or...

Stop it! he thought harshly. Nothing like that happened. He heard his heart beat once in his ears, and the return thought came. Yet.

"Bobby!" he cried, and his voice sounded somehow hollow and echoic, like that travel guide sounded the year Dad took them all to Howe Caverns in New York. Where were they?

In a basement, you doof, his mind answered. You fell, remember?

"Oh yeah," he whispered to himself distractedly, and then another sound came to him. Was it breathing? Bobby, maybe? Johnny cocked his head in the dark room. The sound was light, rapid, barely audible, but it was there. Smiling grimly, Johnny stood, then immediately fell back to the ground. Pain shot through his leg like a bullet. Tears stood out suddenly in his eyes. Had he broken something when he hit ground? Was that possible?

"No," he moaned. "God, no."

There was no way to know for sure until he tried to stand again. His leg hurt a lot less when he was sitting, so maybe there was some hope. Tentatively, he moved one arm over to the left side of his body, next to the hurt leg. The ground beneath his hands was cold, hard ... and somehow yielding. He arched his hands, moving them up on their points like weird, five-legged animals. His fingernails sunk down, just a little. Dirt? Johnny thought. Why would there be dirt down here? He shook his head, deciding he wouldn't know unless a light came on. Bending the knee of his other leg and pushing up with his palms on the ground, Johnny managed to get into a low crouching position. The pain in his left leg flared, but it was nothing he couldn't handle. Not a break, then, maybe only a light sprain. Very slowly, he moved to stand, and the pain bit in a little more, but it wasn't as bad as it could have been. He imagined the large bones in his leg snapping and breaking through the skin, sending gushers of blood...

"Stop it!" he whisper-barked. He stood still for a second, listening with his eyes closed for the sound of breathing again, as if closing his eyes would help him to hear better. His heartbeat dominated his hearing, and following closely, the sound of moths fluttering their wings in the inky black. A shudder wracked through him as he suppressed the memory of Chip, clutching the side of the glass, choking to death. He was about to yell at himself to stop it, louder this time, when a light came on.

Through the lids of his eyes, Johnny saw nothing but a vague yellow and the white under-images that always zipped around when his eyes were closed. He was scared of that light. When lights came on in this crazyhouse, bad stuff always followed. Still, he could hear the moths flapping swifter now, and it he had to run, or beat them off, he'd need to see them. Plus, there was still Bobby to worry about, Bobby who he could hear breathing but who wouldn't answer when he called.

Slowly, Johnny let the bottom part of his eyelids flutter open. More light filtered in, temporarily hurting his eyes. He brought up a hand to shield them, and opened his eyes further. He was looking right at the light—it was a sunlamp like Mom had in the greenhouse in their backyard—and the moths battering themselves against the high-intensity bulbs crazily. There weren't a lot yet, and Johnny some relief in his heart. He removed his hand from his eyes and turned to the right, looking for Bobby. Instead, he came face-to-face with a gray, rotting human skull perched atop some large stick. Moths crawled in the eye sockets and out the nose-hole like contented bees in a nest. The lower half of the skull's jaw had fallen off at some point, and the top half jutted out in a type on angry sneer. John stared at it for a full thirty seconds, unable to breathe, to speak, to scream. Then, a moth flew out and landed on Johnny's face.

Hysterics gripped him and he turned to run, his eyes involuntarily squeezing shut and his arms flailing wildly. He crashed into something and his eyes flew open at once, just in time to see another skewered skull topple from its resting place and shatter noisily on the cold cellar ground. For a second, Johnny stopped screaming, unable to believe that he had just seen what he did. When he tried to start again, his frozen mind allowing at least that, what came out was a series of horse, choking gasps. Johnny turned. He saw four more of the skulls on sticks, set into the earth of a small basement garden. A rotting clump of tomatoes stood pungently next to a large stone wall that served as the back end of the garden. Moths permeated the air but did not fill it; they didn't seem as much of a threat down here as they had upstairs. The skulls, though, staring out at him with idiot eyes, and he saw for the first time that all of them were small. Were they all the skulls of children?

Below him and to the left, he heard a low, groggy moaning and he leaped up, terrified. It's one of the kids' ghosts, he thought. Forget the moths, it's the ghosts that are going to kill me, kill me because I'm alive and they're dead. This thought shot through his head in under a second, and when he did look back, albeit involuntarily, he saw it was a kid. The kid was not dead, though. It was Bobby, lying on the hard-packed ground of the garden, writhing in the dirt and finally coming to.

"Bobby?" he asked momentarily able to ignore the macabre garden around him. "Bobby, you awake?"

His friend, who had landed splayed out on his back on the hard-packed earth, rolled over a little, squeezing his eyes closed even more.

"Bobby, please," Johnny pleaded, wondering if maybe Bobby wasn't in a coma or something like they went into on TV. Christ, what would he do then? He touched a toe to Bobby's side and nudged him. "Come on, Bob."

Johnny leaned down, keeping his mind on Bobby only, grabbed him by the shoulder and gave him a brief shake. He was about to tell him to wake up again when Bobby's eyes flew open, blazing blue and staring.

"Jesus, Bobby, I thought you were in a c—" he began, but then Bobby began screaming. His eyes went even wider, and he raised an arm to point at something behind Johnny. Johnny whirled around and again saw one of the skulls, appearing to look down at them from its perch with wide, uncaring eyes. For a moment, Johnny wanted to scream with Bobby, scream his head off again at this horror show turned reality ... but then the moment passed. Johnny knew he was still scared, still terrified, but for right now at least, he felt he could handle a bunch of skulls. They'd seen one coming into Scary World, right? They weren't anything but parts of people, and they couldn't hurt you.

Unless their ghosts... his mind began fervently, and he surprised himself by shutting that voice down. But this isn't their ghosts, he combated, smiling grimly. It's just a bunch of dumb skulls.

He turned back, and grabbed Bobby by the shoulders. His friend's horrified, contorted face made Johnny want to burst into tears, but he held them back.

"Bobby, listen to me," he said in a firm, almost grownup voice. Bobby went on wailing, turning slightly and pointing at the other skulls standing on their stalks around them. "It's just a bunch of skulls, Bobby." That only seemed to make Bobby scream louder. Desperation clouded Johnny's brain. He wanted to get out of here more than anything, but he refused to do it without Bobby. His friend wasn't going to end up like those kids who had been reduced to skulls in some moldy basement. Or like Chip. Jesus.

Johnny moved himself into a standing position, his leg still crying out in pain but not exactly screaming. He bent, getting Bobby under the armpits, and lifted him up off the ground. He had never been much stronger than Bobby physically, but his adrenaline was pumping furiously now. Still keeping Bobby off the ground, he ran forward and pushed his friend against the stone wall near at the end of the garden. Bobby stopped screaming immediately.

"Are you done?" Johnny yelled at him. Bobby, whose face looked even more scared now than it had when he had first glimpsed the skulls, nodded. His face scrunched up as if he were going to cry. Johnny understood how he felt, but couldn't allow it.

"Bobby, we need to get out of here. Do you understand that?" Bobby nodded again. "Okay, good. 'Cause that guy that brought us here is going to keep doing stuff to us until we get out. We can't let it get to us, okay?"

He watched a single tear fall from one of Bobby's eyes. In a very small voice, Bobby said, "But what about Chip?"

Johnny's heart did a weird little flip-flop. Mustering all the strength he could, wanting again to cry himself, he said, "Chip is dead, Bobby. But if we keep thinking about that, LaRue is going to win and kill us, too. We can't let him."

As if on cue, a booming voice oozing with chilling dark humor spoke from somewhere up above:

"Welcome young boys,
I hope you like my collection of friends
up on those spikes
You'll never escape
no matter what you do
and soon your heads
will be here, too."

Bobby's eyes had been growing wider and wider, and now he hitched in a breath to scream. Johnny clamped a hand over his mouth and muffled it just before it came.

"Don't you get it?" Johnny asked harshly. "That's what he wants! He wants us to go crazy so it'll be easier to … to kill us!"

Bobby's eyes were still wide, but the yelling behind Johnny's hand had stopped. Slowly, Johnny lowered his hand and looked his friend in the eyes. "We have to stick together, Bobby."

"I don't want to die," Bobby said in a quavering, small voice.

"I don't either, man. We're gonna get out of here."

Bobby asked, "Do you promise?" Something inside Johnny clicked over when Bobby asked it. Do I promise? That was a question you asked a grownup. I can't promise stuff like that, I'm only a kid.

Then he thought of the somehow adult voice he had summoned when he pushed Bobby against the wall. How he'd been able to block out the memory of Chip's death, and rationalize the skulls with himself. What if he was an adult now? What did that mean?

"Yes," Johnny said after a moment's hesitation. "Yes, I promise."

"Thank you," Bobby said, and Johnny wanted to cry all over again.

He looked around the room a minute or so later. The skulls had lost their effect. Johnny supposed you could get used to anything if you put your mind to it. Walking over to one of them, slapping moths out of his way, Johnny thought there was something weird about the stakes that held them in place.

Not stakes, he thought, coming closer. Tools.

He touched one of them. It shifted slightly in the dirt, and Johnny thought for a second that it was going to topple. When it didn't, Johnny breathed a brief sigh of relief. Steeling himself, he reached forward, and put his hands on either side of the rotting skull.

"What are you doing?" Bobby barked from behind him, startling him. His hands jumped up and he almost dropped the skull, but in the end held firm. Moths burst from the head like weird flying brain matter. Revulsion gripped Johnny's insides and he felt like he would throw up again. For some reason, he could deal with the skulls, but the moths still frightened him. He glanced around and saw that there were more moths here than there had been when the light first came on. A lot more.

We have to get out of here before something bad happens, he thought. To Bobby he said, "I think these are tools. We might need them."

"Ugh," Bobby said, but didn't turn away as Johnny removed the skull and placed it carefully on the dirt. With both hands, he gripped the long stick the skull had been on and forcefully wrenched it from the earth below his feet. It came out with surprising ease: a six-pronged rake caked with dirt from the lower part of the handle down.

He handed it to Bobby, who looked queasy just touching it, but who continued to hold on to it. Good, Johnny thought. He went to another, picked the skull off, and found this one to be a shovel. He went to a third, and Bobby spoke up: "Johnny, I don't think I can carry more than one of these."

Johnny placed his hands on a third skull. "I know," he said, turning away and closing his eyes when the moths flew out at him. "But I want to take them off anyway. They shouldn't be here."

When the work was done, he stood in the at the edge of the sunlamp's glow, looking into the darkness further off into the basement. He thought he could make out a door back there, but he wasn't quite sure. Moths choked the air now. They needed to move.

He'd unwound his belt and folded it into his back pocket. Tucked into one of the loops at his side was a hammer he had found at the end of the garden. He held the shovel, a little large to carry around easily, in his left hand. Behind him, Bobby held the rake, a little smaller but still somewhat awkward. Johnny's eyes flicked left and right, surveying the dark they were about to enter into. Nothing registered except for the slow, steady hum of the moths flapping their wings. The moths, the damned moths.

He turned around and slowly traversed the dead garden. "What are you doing?" Bobby asked, but Johnny didn't answer him. His insides felt somehow cold now, his mind quiet. Was this what being a grownup felt like? He didn't really want to know.

The sunlamp hung from the corner of the low basement ceiling, shining hotly down upon him. Johnny stared up into the light for a second, twisting the handle of the shovel in his small hands, slicking it with his sweat. Then, calling up memories of last spring's Little League season, he slung the shovel over his shoulder like he had gripped that Louisville Slugger the day the Sharks beat the Lions. Slitting his eyes against the glare of the lamp, he swung out and up, shattering the glass bulb. A distinctly electric pop sound perforated the air, and several small sparks flew. Behind him, Bobby uttered a small cry.

Now he could still hear the moths, but he couldn't see them. That was something, wasn't it?

He also can't see us, Johnny thought. He wasn't aware that the thought was going to hit him until it did. For a moment, it gave him pause: how had LaRue been able to see them? He knew everywhere they went, added what they did into his creepy little rhymes. Were there cameras? There seemed to be speakers everywhere, projecting LaRue's crazy voice. Why not cameras?

That didn't matter now. What mattered was getting out of this madhouse. Alive, if possible.

He turned, stepping forward gingerly, favoring the leg that still hurt a little. "Come on," he said, his foot landed in something soft and squishy; some type of vegetable, most likely. It didn't matter, not now. He continued on, making sure he could hear Bobby's breathing behind him in the dark, dark room, feeling ahead of himself with the shovel the way a blind person would use a cane. Moments later, he bumped his shoulder against the edge of something, what felt like a door, the one he'd thought he could see when the light had still been on.

"Watch out," he whispered back to Bobby. There's a doorway here.

"Okay," Bobby whispered back, not sounding as scared as he probably felt. Good for you, Bobby, he thought, smiling a bit ruefully.

I wish I could see where we were, he thought, and as if LaRue had read his mind, a high-intensity light came on just above his head. Behind him, Bobby gasped. Moths flew toward the light like starving men shown a feast. Johnny glanced up, an icy splinter of fear poking into his heart. The similarly cold voice of Etienne LaRue spoke up, but the voice sounded slightly distant, as if the speakers weren't that close anymore.

"I see you
can you see me?
Stop now, dear boys
You'll never be free."

"That's what you think," Johnny said quietly, glancing around briefly. They were in some sort of pantry. Handmade wooden shelves dominated the walls down here, and dozens and dozens of cans and jars stuffed the shelves. Most of the jars seemed to be filled with homemade jam. A scary sort of longing gripped Johnny suddenly. Grandma makes jam sometimes, his mind announced irrationally. Will I ever see her again?

Sadness threatened to break Johnny's stoic façade, but he refused to let it. He couldn't let Bobby see him breaking down, that more than anything. Instead, he swung the shovel upward, smashing this light, too. The smell of ozone filled the air, as well as the sickening, somehow muddy smell of moths being burned alive.

As the residue of the light filtered out of the darkness, Johnny thought he saw another small shaft of light up ahead. Not the artificial high-intensity lamps that LaRue kept flipping on, but what seemed like natural light. Outside light.

"Is that…?" he began, but then Bobby burst into a shrill cry behind him.

"That's out!" Bobby pushed him aside as he ran forward, toward what really did look like out. Johnny moved to run after him, when fear gripped him. What if it was a trap? What if it was like the room where Chip was killed?

"Bobby, stop!" he yelled, but Bobby kept running, calling out, "That's out, that's out, we made it out!"

Slowly, carefully, Johnny followed. He could see Bobby's silhouette now, outlined by the light coming in through a square pane somewhere up ahead. The silhouette stopped up ahead, and from where he was Johnny could hear Bobby call out, "It's a door out!" with unmitigated glee.

Johnny willed himself not to run. It could still be a trap. Sharp things could come out of nowhere to chop their heads off. Still, excitement bubbled in his brain. Bobby had found a door out, and they could finally escape. Johnny hoped it wasn't too good to be true.

As he came closer to his friend, he realized with mounting dismay that, yes, it was too good to be true. Even before Bobby spoke another word, Johnny understood. LaRue wouldn't let them off this easy. He probably still had plans for them.

When he reached the door, Bobby was pulling at the handle, twisting it back and forth. The top half of the door was divided into four small panes of glass, separated by a plus-sign of wood in the center, kind of like one of those old-fashioned windows Grandma had at her house. The bad news was that the small windows had been fitted with cast-iron bars, situated so close together that Johnny didn't think he could even get his hand through them.

The door, of course, was locked.

No fancy traps, Johnny thought, peering through the unreachable windows. Far off, he could see some bright lights dancing in the night. The lights of Scary World. They were really that close to other people, but they were trapped here like animals. How long had it taken them to walk over here from what Johnny remembered as the perimeter of the park? Ten minutes? Ten minutes away and already one of them was dead.

"Jesus," Johnny barked, for the moment unable to think about anything but the hope of escape so close, only to be yanked away. No fancy traps, he thought again, he doesn't need that here. He just needs us to see the lights of outside and he knows it makes it easier to hurt us. Well, dammit, he's right. This hurts more than anything.

"Let's go," he said tiredly to Bobby, expecting another incident of shrieking and crying to rival the moment Bobby awoke to see the skulls. Off to the left there was another dark corridor, and Johnny trudged in that direction, steeling himself for the outburst. Instead, there was bare silence. He looked back for confirmation that his friend was following him, and stopped. Bobby was staring out at the bright lights of the theme park they had been led from. He wasn't crying, or going into hysterics, as Johnny had thought. Only staring. "Bobby?" he asked.

A year before, Bobby, Chip and Johnny were in Chip's treehouse, hanging out and reading comics. No one wanted to talk about what was so obviously on all their minds. A week before, Bobby's father had been killed in a bus accident commuting home from work. Bobby, who could be as loud as Chip if you really got him going, had been pretty quiet since then. The air in the clubhouse that day felt so thick, like it was that beef stew Johnny's Mom made once in a while. Without warning, Bobby put his comic down—Batman, his favorite—stared at the two of them with glassy eyes, and said in a flat, cold voice, "I'm gonna die. You two are, too. Everyone. We're all gonna die." Then, he picked up his comic and began reading again.

Now, as Bobby looked out the window, a window that could have meant freedom, Johnny watched the amusement park lights play over those same glassy eyes. And in that eerily adult voice, Bobby said, "We're never getting out of this house."

"Bobby, no," Johnny said, putting his arm out. Bobby didn't shake it off, but Johnny felt some cold chill grasp him and he lowered his arm.

"You saw what happened to Chip. It's gonna happen to us, too. Me and you. We're gonna die in here."

"Not if we keep moving, Bobby. Maybe if we get upstairs…"

"You promised me, back there. You promised me that we would get out."

Johnny stared at his friend, a little scared. There was hate in Bobby's voice. Hate, not against LaRue or the house or the situation. Hate against him.

"I meant it, too, Bobby," he said, trying on a smile he knew felt fake.

"Liar," Bobby said in that same emotionless voice. It was chilling in a way that the skulls and the moths weren't. Those were new things, scary things in this suddenly scary world. But this was Bobby, a kid he'd known since kindergarten. His world had turned dark and scary and that was okay, not great, but okay. But not Bobby. Not now.

He was about to say something, anything to smooth things over and get them going again, when Bobby suddenly moved, brushing past him down the dark corridor. Without allowing himself to think, Bobby followed behind blindly, not daring to speak.

What if his promise was a lie?

More stairs, but for some reason these seemed more solid. Johnny tapped a step with the shovel a little ways up. In the darkness, he saw a brief, fiery spark.

"Concrete," he muttered.

"Okay," Bobby said. Johnny didn't detect the cold grownup voice there, and that made him feel a little better. Not much, but a little. "You ready?"

"Yeah," Johnny responded, feeling ahead with his shovel to find the first step again. "Keep against the wall and keep feeling ahead with your rake." Bobby grunted something Johnny assumed he had to take as "All right."

He heard Bobby's sneakers skiffle on the gritty surface of the step just above him. Johnny followed nervously. The memory of the last time he and Bobby were on stairs together was still fresh in his mind. One hand on the shovel, feeling ahead, and one hand on the wall, he slowly ascended the stairs. Nervousness simmered in his stomach.

A few moments later, he heard Bobby say from above him, "I'm at a door!"

Emotions bounced like superballs throughout his insides. Was this another trap? Could this be a way out? What was behind door number one?

"Wait for me!" he called up, and then he was there, touching what felt like a wooden surface. "It's heavy," he whispered to Bobby, placing his ear against the door. "I can't hear anything on the other side."

"You think it's another trap, like with Chip?"

"It could be," Johnny said, feeling around for the knob and finally finding it. There was silence for a second.

"I think I got something," Bobby said, sounding a lot less like the unfeeling boy down at the basement door, but not exactly like his old self again. His old self is gone, Johnny, you know that. His mind whispered. Yours, too. You can't be children like that again.

Johnny closed his eyes and said, "What?"

"How about we open the door and stand off to both sides. That way, if something comes at us, we can stay back and it won't hurt us."

Johnny couldn't really think of any problems with this idea, and since it seemed to be the only thing to do, he agreed.

"All right, count to three," he said to Johnny. Johnny nodded, smiled when he realized Bobby couldn't see him, and said, "One, two, three!"

Johnny grabbed the knob, turned it violently toward him and pushed the door open in one swift maneuver. For a moment, nothing moved. Then, the dark, terrifying voice of their unseen host spoke up over an equally hidden loudspeaker.

"Now you both know my little pets
and seen it when I feed them
but now you've found their special place
for this is where I breed them!"

"Oh shit," Bobby said, and the moths came from everywhere.

Johnny threw his arms up in the now-familiar warding-off pose, his shovel dropping and clanging to the ground. Between his closed arms, he could see into the room beyond the door. Obviously once a kitchen, this room now housed what seemed like millions of moths, all swarming in the blue hues of black lights toward them. He couldn't make much else out; what seemed like a small stand of trees and a few large piles of rocks stood against the walls of this former kitchen, but the moths choked his vision as surely as they had choked Chip's lungs.

Bobby stood across from him, high, girlish shrieks peeling out of him. It was almost impossible to hear over the thousands of wings flapping furiously past them. Johnny turned, panicked, to stare at Bobby, and saw a moth bullet into his open mouth.

Not again! Johnny thought, his heart popping a bit in his chest. He bowed his head a little and stepped across to Bobby, who was spitting out the moth out onto the floor. Johnny glanced down and saw the thing, ugly and brown, squirming sluggishly on the stair at Bobby's feet. Johnny stepped forward, squashing the moth under his sneaker, and blocking Bobby's mouth with one of his hands. His other hand was clamping his own nose shut. Leaning closer to Bobby's ear, Johnny opened his mouth slightly and yelled, "Keep your mouth and nose blocked! They can get in!"

He pulled back to see Bobby nodding frantically, and let go of him. Bobby ducked his head a little, throwing his arm over his eyes. His rake fell from his hands and leaned drunkenly against the doorframe. Immediately, he plugged his own nose and kept his mouth shut the way you did when you were demonstrating that you were going to keep a secret. Bobby's lips were sealed.

He was also looking out into the kitchen, his eyes wide with shock. Johnny could almost hear him thinking about Chip. Hell, it was hard not to. It took him a second to tear Bobby's attention away from the incoming moths. When he finally touched Bobby on the shoulder, his friend wheeled around and stared at him the same way. Bobby flicked his eyes toward the kitchen. There was probably a door out of the moth-room, and if there was, Johnny intended to get on the other side of it. After that, he didn't know, but they certainly couldn't go back down the cellar stairs, where the skulls were. The skulls, and little else.

Bobby finally got his meaning. He shook his head no, squeezing his eyes shut. You can't make me, the gesture said.

Johnny opened his eyes wider, cocking his head toward the door. Anger was fighting panic in both his gut and his brain. Can't make you, huh?

Again, Bobby shook his head, closing his arms tighter over his face. The moths deflected off the clenched arms like bullets shot against hard stone. "Stop it!" Bobby yelled, sounding panicked. "Please stop it!"

Johnny stepped toward Bobby again, letting go of his nose and grabbing Bobby by the sleeve. I don't think he's angry anymore, just scared, Johnny thought, for some reason feeling sad. Bobby had been a little unbearable when he was mad, but scared he was a challenge. And, Johnny thought, he really didn't need any more challenges tonight.

He leaned close to Bobby's ear. "I'm going in there!" he shouted. "I think there's a door at the edge of the kitchen! You can come or you can stay, but I'm going!"

Bobby turned, glaring at Johnny through his encircling arms. Angry again, Bobby thought, some vague relief creeping into him. "Let's go," he said, ducking his head and letting go of Bobby as he turned into the giant flurry of moths. He glanced down long enough to locate his dropped shovel, and hold it across his chest like a soldier with a rifle.

Then, he was off, racing right into the heart of Moth Country. Beside him, obscured by the storm of dive-bombing moths, a small forest of potted plants flickered by. Stands of rocks were scattered throughout, and Johnny narrowly missed tripping over one. In the dim neon of the black light, Johnny squinted to see better ahead of him. He had been right. Tucked into the last space of west wall up ahead was a large wooden door with two giant, but dead, spotlights situated over it. It was closed, sure, but closed didn't always mean locked, right?

In this house it does, his traitorous mind whispered, and he tried hard to ignore it.

A particularly dense swarm of moths came toward him, and Johnny realized almost too late that he'd left his nose and mouth completely exposed. Acting on reflex alone, Johnny stopped and slammed the shovel into the air, battering the swarm back. A small group of tinny bong! sounds reverberated in the close air space just above him. A tiny rain of dead moths showered down upon his head. He didn't even bother to shake them off. Moving the shovel back across his chest, Johnny got moving again.

Something large brushed past him on the left. He cried out, at once terrified. Visions of giant killer moths danced in his head. Then, he saw Bobby rushing ahead of him, holding his rake as Johnny was holding the shovel. It's like one of those horror movies from the 50's Dad likes, Johnny thought, The Army Boys and the Killer Moth Invasion. And, despite everything that had happened and everything that was happening around him, Johnny began to giggle.

He reached the door a few seconds after Bobby, who was holding the rake under his arm and blocking his mouth and nose with his hands.

"What's so funny?" Bobby asked, his voice muffled: Whz zo unny? That only made Johnny laugh harder, grabbing the door frame and bending over. His mind screamed at him: You're at the door, you idiot, go! Go! But for the moment, he couldn't. This laughter, hysterical as it was, felt like the first taste of food a starving man takes. He clung to it desperately. If he could still laugh, he was still alive.

Eventually, he looked up, blocking his nose and mouth, and saw Bobby laughing, too, his body shaking in the dark light. Take that LaRue, he thought, the laughs finally tapering off. You didn't get us all the way.

Bobby removed his hand from his mouth. "Stand to the side," he said, smiling a little. Johnny did and Bobby reached forward and pulled the door open.

"Huh?" Johnny asked. What the hell...?

Bobby stood by his side, gripping the rake in both hands. "What is it?"

The door stood open, the boys peering in, confused. The doorframe had been divided down the middle by what looked like a thin plaster wall. The black lighting behind them didn't extend very far into the dual rooms, but Johnny guessed the wall went all the way from the raised jamb to the very back wall. Johnny opened his mouth to answer Bobby, when the terribly familiar voice of Etienne LaRue boomed over their heads.

"Time to choose, my dear young boys!
left or right, it's quite a choice
you're safe from harm if you pick correct
but choosing wrong means certain death!"

"I hate him," Bobby said.

"Me too," Johnny agreed, and then the two large spotlights slammed on above them. Slowly, the boys turned. The moths, which had been annoying but not really a threat, now made a beeline to the lights ... and the boys underneath.

Or a mothline, Johnny thought and an insane urge to start laughing again gripped him. He fought it back, turning from the moths and screaming, "Come on!" to Bobby. On instinct, he bolted through the left side of the door, grabbing the doorknob behind him with the hand not holding his shovel. The glow from both the black lights and the spotlight cut off immediately. The bottom of the door stood snug up against the jamb, making the darkness complete.

A moth or two battered against the back of his head, and he brushed them away. "Bobby?" he asked, and there was no response. He called it louder: "Bobby!"

Then, muffled, he heard the reply. "Johnny!" Quietly, Johnny moved through the dark toward the plaster wall. "Bobby? You over there?"

"Yes! It doesn't go far back—there's like a brick wall all around me."

Shit, Johnny thought. Divide us and trap him. Kind of dried up the giggles, LaRue.

"Okay, no problem," Johnny called over. "I'll just open up the door and you can slide over, okay?"

Johnny felt his way along the wall, feeling it along with the palm of one hand, gripping the shovel with his other. Within a moment, he reached the door, and felt around until he found the doorknob. He twisted it. His wet palm slicked over it, but it stayed still. Frowning, looking down in the dark at where his hand was, he turned the knob the other way. It gave slightly, then stopped.

"Oh no," Johnny muttered. "Oh no no no." Please tell me it doesn't lock from the other side, he thought. Please God.

He turned it again, back, forth. Suddenly frantic, he dropped the shovel and threw his shoulder against the door. Bright, electric pain sizzled in Johnny's arm, but the door didn't budge.

"Bobby," he said, "We have a little problem."

"Oh God!" he heard Bobby bark from the other side of the wall.

Johnny told him, "No, no, don't worry, let me think about this for a second."

"Johnny, help me!" Bobby cried from the other side of the wall.

"Don't panic yet," Johnny called distractedly. "I'll get you out of there." He was about to think of how he could do just that when Bobby called back in a high, squeaky shriek.

"He turned on hoses somewhere!"

Hoses? "Hoses?"

"They're coming from the ceiling! It's filling up with water, Johnny!" Bobby cried. "I'm in a box and it's filling up with water!"

"Oh my God," Bobby said in a hushed, amazed voice. From somewhere above, Johnny could hear the low, scuttery giggle of Etienne LaRue, and all the blood inside him turned to ice.

He's going to drown, here, Johnny thought, inside this house. First Chip, now Bobby, and I'll be here all alone in this dark house.

"No!" Johnny screamed, dropping his shovel. "No, it's not fair!" Howling, he battered the wall in front of him with his angry fists, punctuating each pound with an increasingly desperate "No!"

From the other side of the wall, Bobby started to scream, as if the sound of Johnny's wails was infectious. "It's getting higher!" Bobby wailed, sounding more terrified than ever. "Oh God, help me!"

In frustration, Johnny slammed his fist one last time against the wall. Something jumped out at his face and he screamed, terrified that the moths in the kitchen had found a way in here. But it wasn't moths. Johnny rubbed two fingers down his hot, sweaty cheek, a surprised awe dawning in his mind. Not moths. Plaster-dust.

"Johnny!" Bobby yelled.

"Use your rake!" Johnny called, feeling around for his shovel. "The wall's plaster! You can break through!"

"What?" Bobby called back. He sounded out of breath. Was he treading water? "Shit," Johnny muttered, his hand finally landing on the shovel's handle. Grunting, he picked it up, holding like a bayonet.

"Stand back!" he called, and thrust the shovel forward. The blade sunk into the plaster wall with surprising ease. Smiling maniacally, Johnny wrenched it out of the wall and thrust forward again. When he pulled it out this time, he yanked it up, pulling a large hunk of plaster out with it. When it fell away, Johnny felt the wall where he had cut through. There was a large, gaping hole in the center, and when he ran his finger along the rim, more plaster-dust sifted down.

Why isn't water coming through? he wondered frantically. It should be coming through, I busted through the wall. He lifted the shovel and threaded it experimentally through his hole. It went in a few inches, then stopped, the blade hitting resistance. It's not a solid wall, he thought, reading the shovel again, it's hollow.

"Look out, Bobby!" he called, but there was no answer. He paused. "Bobby?" Nothing.

"Oh God," he said, slamming the shovel through the hole and into the wall on the other side. It was like putting a knife through semi-hard butter. Water squirted out of the new hole and onto Johnny's legs. He moved back a little, trying to avoid the flow and pushed the shovel through again. Now, the other side of the wall burst open, water gushing out onto the floor and soaking his sneakers. He heard a meaty thump against that side of the wall. Bobby.

"Bobby!" he called out, trying to climb through the hole. The gushing water prevented him, and he stood back, wanting to bang his fists against something else. Soon, the sound of the water splashing against the floor lessened, and Johnny lurched forward, climbing into the hole and through to the other room.

"Bobby?" he asked, and his knee encountered something soft and wet. Bobby's leg? To his left, he heard a small "Ow."

"Bobby?" he asked again.

"I hit my head against the wall," Bobby said, sounding tired and very young. It seemed like he would say something else, but then let out a series of waterlogged coughs.

"You okay, man?" Johnny asked, reaching out and slapping Bobby on the back. He had a fleeting memory of his Mom doing that to him when he had almost drowned in Grandma's pool when he was five. His insides clenched at the thought of his Mom. All at once, he desperately wanted to see her again.

"I'm wet," he said simply. "And I want to go home."

"Okay," Johnny said, then surprised himself by grabbing Bobby, and pulling him into a hug. Bobby stiffened for a moment, then hugged Johnny back. Fresh tears sprung up in Johnny's eyes. "I thought you were gonna die," Johnny said.

"I thought so, too," Bobby said, and it sounded like he was crying, too.

They stayed like that for a full minute, cold and wet in the dark, but feeling better than they had since they first stepped into this bad, bad house.

They were standing at the end of the empty room opposite the plaster-wall, feeling husked out and tired, but otherwise all right. There was another set of stairs here, reaching up into that unknown darkness.

"You wanna go up?" Johnny asked.

"Do we have a choice?" Bobby answered. He sounded old now. Johnny didn't need to answer him. He began climbing, Bobby following close behind. When they reached the top, Johnny wasn't surprised to find another door. He sighed.

"Same drill?" he asked.

"Yeah."

Johnny backed up against the banister on his side, and heard Bobby scoot up against the wall on his. "On three: one, two, three." He twisted the doorknob and flung the door open, squinting his eyes against whatever might come at them.

Nothing came at them. Johnny opened his eyes and wasn't very surprised to see that they had come back to the second-story hallway, the one that led to the room where Chip was killed. Dim light came from the other end of the hallway, where the other set of stairs had nearly killed them him. For a second, he wondered if he should just give up. They were only going around and around in circles, and LaRue would get them when they were too worn out to fight back anymore.

Then he looked up, and saw something from this vantage point he hadn't seen before. A trap door set into the ceiling. A trap door that led into the attic.

Snapshots of memory flashed through his mind: the bags of moths dropping from the ceiling, the hoses coming from above. Excitement leapt into Johnny's heart, but it was of a dark sort. He leaned close to Bobby, aware that if LaRue could track their movements, he might also be able to hear them.

He whispered, "LaRue is up there, in the attic." Bobby looked up, then looked back at Johnny, nodding. "He's probably got the keys to this place."

"How are we supposed to get up there?" he asked. "And won't he see us?"

Johnny glanced up at the trap door again, noticing the small pull-rope with a large knot at the end of it. "We can get up," he said, turning back to his friend. "As for him seeing us, I don't know. You said it. We don't really have a choice."

Bobby nodded again. "Okay," he said. "How do we get up there?"

"Give me your rake." They traded tools and stepped out of the doorway, Johnny looking up. Stretching, holding the rake by the end of the handle, he was able to get the knot between two of the tines. As he was about to pull, a bright, blinding light slammed on over one of the doors. Almost immediately, moths that had been fluttering around the hallway aimlessly went for the light. LaRue's voice came from somewhere up above.

"For all the things you've seen and feared
Nothing's worse than what's up here!"

"Whatever," Johnny muttered.

His eyes became accustomed to the light, and he looked in that direction. Behind the light he saw what looked like a small speaker. A foot away from that, a small black object hummed like a fat electronic bee. Its one large glass eye stared at Johnny, humming as it focused. A video camera.

Bobby had followed Johnny's gaze. Now, he smiled and stuck his middle finger up at the camera's unblinking eye. Johnny grunted, pulling the rake down. The trap door creaked open a little. Johnny yanked down, harder this time, and it opened more. Bobby stepped forward, standing on his tiptoes and grasping the rake higher up. On three, they heaved the rake down together, and the door came swinging open, a segmented stepladder on tracks sliding down and connecting with the floor. The boys looked up. LaRue was up there, staring down at them.

He looked as if he were about to speak, but then reached behind him and brought out a small canvas sack. Johnny knew what was in the bag, but found he wasn't much scared anymore. In a world of moths, a canvas bag full of them doesn't much have the power to frighten after a while. He turned to Bobby, switching tools back, and looked up again.

LaRue hurled the sack down at him. It landed on his head, sending moths flying everywhere. Johnny flung the bag away, then mounted the steps. Above, LaRue issued a small grunt of surprise and reached behind him for another bag. Johnny peeled back his lips and gritted his teeth, so the moths couldn't get in. A few flew at his teeth, but deflected off. Holding the shovel in one hand, he began to climb. Another bag landed on his head and slid off. More moths fluttered out, but Johnny didn't care. If LaRue had the key out of this spookhouse, he was going to get it.

"No!" LaRue said, throwing down another bag. Couldn't think of a rhyme for that, LaRue? Johnny thought darkly, and continued to climb. When he looked up next, his teeth together in a wide Cheshire smile, LaRue was gone.

Johnny poked his head up through the hole, looking around, very wary of LaRue. The attic was very well lit. In the corner, four large generators stood like those rocks from Stonehenge, looking alien in this decrepit place. A wooden wall cut the attic in half, a doorless doorway standing in the center of it. Johnny climbed up the rest of the stairs, shaking his shovel back and forth to clear the scourge of moths. One plugged up his nose and twittered there. Revulsion turned his stomach, but he didn't panic. He stood to the side of the hole in the floor, pressed the other side of his nose shut, and exhaled sharply. The moth flew out drunkenly, falling to the floor.

Bobby's head came into view, his right hand holding his rake straight out, his arm blocking his nose and mouth. He joined Johnny at the top. Johnny pointed to the door, and Bobby nodded. Johnny stepped closer to the door, only slightly afraid, and peeked in. Etienne LaRue was in there, all right. And he was trying to climb out a window.

Johnny bellowed. A sudden, furious burst of rage overtook him, and he rushed forward. "No way!" he yelled, traversing the attic room past the bank of small black and white TV screens. LaRue's large top hat stood atop one of the screens like a cast-off from the Mad Hatter. Johnny leapt forward, reaching out, and grabbed LaRue's hair before his head could disappear from sight. The man cried out.

"Get back in here," Johnny said, knowing that he sounded more grown up than ever. This man had made his voice that way. This man had done a lot worse than that tonight.

"No!" LaRue whined. Johnny hoisted LaRue's head up, dropping his shovel, and slapping the man across the face. One of the window's gauzy white curtains fluttered toward him and he moved it back with his head.

"Get back in here," he repeated, growling his words. Bobby came toward them and placed the heavy steel tines of the rake against the top of LaRue's skull.

"Want me to dig it in?" Bobby asked.

"Okay, okay!" LaRue said, sounding terrified. Johnny watched him clamber back in, bending down to grab the shovel again. Bobby held the rake points to the man's neck, staring at him with wide, hateful eyes. When LaRue was back in, Johnny stood before him, smaller than LaRue but feeling much older.

"You killed Chip," he said. "You tried to kill all of us."

LaRue's eyes darted frantically from left to right, as if LaRue was trying to find a way to escape. Johnny didn't like that look. They couldn't escape. Why should he?

Bobby asked from beside him, "Are all those bags filled with moths?" He indicated a large pile in the corner of this room, stacked high with slightly shifting canvas sacks.

"Yes, they...," LaRue began, and then made a mad dash toward Johnny. Working on reflex alone, Johnny lifted his shovel and swung it, connecting the back of the scoop with LaRue's head. The man crumpled to the floor immediately.

"Is he dead?" Bobby asked, standing over him.

"No, he's still breathing." Johnny responded, looking down at LaRue, the author of all this night's horror, and feeling that now-familiar crawling revulsion.

"What should we do?" Bobby asked. Johnny looked down at LaRue, back at the bags of moths, and back at LaRue.

"I have an idea."

LaRue opened his eyes a short time later. Johnny looked down at him and smiled a little when LaRue discovered he couldn't move.

"The hoses," Johnny said, bending closer to the man. "The hoses you tried to drown Bobby with." He smiled again, watching as LaRue tried to break free from the hoses tied around his body. Both he and Bobby had been in the Scouts for two years, and they knew how to tie knots.

"When we were looking through your pockets for the keys, we found this," Bobby said, coming up behind Johnny. Bobby was also smiling. He held up a silver Zippo lighter, and handed it to Johnny.

"What's the name of this place again?" Johnny said, pretending to think hard.

Bobby answered,

"It's not a game,
It's Drawn to the Flame."

Johnny laughed, a little shakily. "Oh yeah, let's do that!

"Poor LaRue is stuck here, too."

Bobby laughed with him.

"We tied him tight, he can't even fight."

"How does it feel, LaRue?" Johnny asked, and then the man began to scream. Bobby reached behind him and lifted a bag full of fluttering moths above LaRue's face. When he upended it, the moths flew out everywhere, at least a dozen flying into LaRue's mouth, cutting off his scream.

The man began to convulse on the floor, and the boys turned away from him. They reached the window and climbed out onto the ladder LaRue had used to reach up at the very beginning of the night. Before he climbed below the bottom of the window, Johnny reached out, flicked on the lighter, and set the thin white curtain ablaze.

Two young boys ran across a dark field toward a carnival that was shut down for the night. There were no more lights ahead of them, but the dead rides and dark booths still meant freedom. They made their way around the perimeter of the park, and by the time they got to the parking lot, they were sobbing.

Behind the park, on a dark hill across a field, an abandoned old house burned. Windows shattered open and old, dry wood charred to the ground below. Swarms of gray insects burst into the night sky, blotting out the stars. The ones who weren't drawn back to the flame flew off in search of better things.

For the moths, the flames meant freedom, too.

THE COMPANION
BY RAMSEY CAMPBELL

WHEN STONE REACHED the fairground, having been misdirected twice, he thought it looked more like a gigantic amusement arcade. A couple of paper cups tumbled and rattled on the shore beneath the promenade, and the cold insinuating October wind scooped the Mersey across the slabs of red rock that formed the beach, across the broken bottles and abandoned tyres. Beneath the stubby white mock turrets of the long fairground façade, shops displayed souvenirs and fish and chips. Among them, in the fairground entrances, scraps of paper whirled.

Stone almost walked away. This wasn't his best holiday. One fairground in Wales had been closed, and this one certainly wasn't what he'd expected. The guidebook had made it sound like a genuine fairground, sideshows you must stride among not looking in case their barkers lured you in, the sudden shock of waterfalls cascading down what looked like painted cardboard, the shots and bells and wooden concussions of target galleries, the girls' shrieks overhead, the slippery armour and juicy crunch of toffee-apples, the illuminations springing alight against a darkening sky. But at least, he thought, he had chosen his time well. If he went in now, he might have the fairground almost to himself.

As he reached an entrance, he saw his mother eating fish and chips from a paper tray. What nonsense! She would never have eaten standing up in public—"like a horse," as she'd used to say. But he watched as she hurried out of the shop, face averted from him and the wind. Of course, it had been the way she ate, with little snatching motions of her fork and mouth. He pushed the incident to the side of his mind in the hope that it would fall away, and hurried through the entrance, into the clamour of colour and noise.

The high roof with its bare iron girders reminded him at once of a railway station, but the place was noisier still. The uproar—the echoing sirens and jets and dangerous groaning of metal—was trapped, and was deafening. It was so overwhelming that he had to remind himself he could see, even if he couldn't hear.

But there wasn't much to see. The machines looked faded and dusty. Cars like huge armchairs were lurching and spinning helplessly along a switchback, a canvas canopy was closing over an endless parade of seats, a great disc tasselled with seats was lifting towards the roof, dangling a lone couple over its gears. With so few people in sight it seemed almost that the machines, frustrated by inaction, were operating themselves. For a moment Stone had the impression of being shut in a dusty room where the toys, as in childhood tales, had come to life.

He shrugged vaguely and turned to leave. Perhaps he could drive to the fairground at Southport, though it was a good few miles across the Mersey. His holiday was dwindling rapidly. He wondered how they were managing at the tax office in his absence. Slower than usual, no doubt.

Then he saw the merry-go-round. It was like a toy forgotten by another child and left here, or handed down the generations.

Beneath its ornate scrolled canopy, the horses rode on poles towards their reflections in a ring of mirrors. The horses were white wood or wood painted white, their bodies dappled with purple, red and green, and some of their sketched faces too. On the hub, above a notice MADE IN AMSTERDAM, an organ piped to itself. Around it, Stone saw carved fish, mermen, zephyrs, a head and shoulders smoking a pipe in a frame, a landscape of hills and lake and unfurling perched hawk. "Oh yes," Stone said.

As he clambered onto the platform he felt a hint of embarrassment, but nobody seemed to be watching. "Can you play me?" said the head in the frame. "My boy's gone for a minute."

The man's hair was the colour of the smoke from his pipe. His lips puckered on the stem and smiled. "It's a good merry-go-round," Stone said.

"You know about them, do you?"

"Well, a little." The man looked disappointed, and Stone hurried on. "I know a lot of fairgrounds. They're my holiday, you see, every year. Each year I cover a different area. I may write a book." The idea had occasionally tempted him—but he hadn't taken notes, and he still had ten years to retirement, for which the book had suggested itself as an activity.

"You go alone every year?"

"It has its merits. Less expensive, for one thing. Helps me save. Before I retire I mean to see Disneyland and Vienna." He thought of the Big Wheel, Harry Lime, the earth falling away beneath. "I'll get on," he said.

He patted the unyielding shoulders of the horse, and remembered a childhood friend who'd had a rocking-horse in his bedroom. Stone had ridden it a few times, more and more wildly when it was nearly time to go home; his friend's bedroom was brighter than his, and as he clung to the wooden shoulders he was clutching the friendly room too. Funny thinking of that now, he thought. Because I haven't been on a merry-go-round for years, I suppose.

The merry-go-round stirred; the horse lifted him, let him sink. As they moved forward, slowly gathering momentum, Stone saw a crowd surging through one of the entrances and spreading through the funfair. He grimaced: it had been his fairground for a little while, they needn't have arrived just as he was enjoying his merry-go-round.

The crowd swung away. A jangle of pinball machines sailed by. Amid the Dodgems a giant with a barrel body was spinning, flapping its limp arms, a red electric cigar thrust in its blank grin and throbbing in time with its slow thick laughter. A tinny voice read Bingo numbers, buzzing indistinctly. Perhaps it was because he hadn't eaten for a while, saving himself for the toffee-apples, but he was growing dizzy—it felt like the whirling blurred shot of the fair in Saturday Night and Sunday Morning, a fair he hadn't liked because it was too grim. Give him Strangers on a Train, Some Came Running, The Third Man, even the fairground murder in Horrors of the Black Museum. He shook his head to try to control his pouring thoughts.

But the fair was spinning faster. The Ghost Train's station raced by, howling and screaming. People strolling past the merry-go-round looked jerky. Here came the Ghost Train once more, and Stone glimpsed the queue beneath the beckoning green corpse. They were staring at him. No, he realised next time 'round, they were staring at the merry-go-round. He was just something that kept appearing as they watched. At the end of the queue, staring and poking around inside his nostrils, stood Stone's father.

Stone gripped the horse's neck as he began to fall. The man was already wandering away towards the Dodgems. Why was his mind so traitorous today? It wouldn't be so bad if the comparisons it made weren't so repulsive. Why, he'd never met a man or woman to compare with his parents. Admired people, yes, but not in the same way. Not since the two polished boxes had been lowered into holes and hidden. Noise and colour spun about him and inside him. Why wasn't he allowing himself to think about his parents' death? He knew why he was blocking, and that should be his salvation: at the age of ten he'd suffered death and hell every night.

He clung to the wood in the whirlpool and remembered. His father had denied him a nightlight and his mother had nodded, saying "Yes, I think it's time." He'd lain in bed, terrified to move in case he betrayed his presence to the darkness, mouthing "Please God don't let it" over and over. He lay so that he could see the faint grey vertical line of the window between the curtains in the far distance, but even that light seemed to be receding. He knew that death and hell would be like this. Sometimes, as he began to blur with sleep and the room grew larger and the shapes dark against the darkness awoke, he couldn't tell that he hadn't already died.

He sat back as the horse slowed and he began to slip forward across its neck. What then? Eventually he'd seen through the self-perpetuating trap of religious guilt, of hell, of not daring to believe in it because then it would get you. For a while he'd been vaguely uneasy in dark places, but not sufficiently so to track down the feeling and conquer it. After a while it had dissipated, along with his parents' overt disapproval of his atheism. Yes, he thought as his memories and the merry-go-round slowed, I was happiest then, lying in bed hearing and feeling them and the house around me. Then, when he was thirty, a telephone call had summoned him to the hole in the road, to the sight of the car like a dead black beetle protruding from the hole. There had been a moment of sheer vertiginous terror, and then it was over. His parents had gone into darkness. That was enough. It was the one almost religious observance he imposed on himself: think no more.

And there was no reason to do so now. He staggered away from the merry-go-round, towards the pinball arcade that occupied most of one side of the funfair. He remembered how,

when he lay mouthing soundless pleas in bed, he would sometimes stop and think of what he'd read about dreams: that they
might last for hours but in reality occupied only a split second.
Was the same true of thoughts? And prayers, when you had
nothing but darkness by which to tell the time? Besides defend-
ing him, his prayers were counting off the moments before
dawn. Perhaps he had used up only a minute, only a second of
darkness. Death and hell—what strange ideas I used to have,
he thought. Especially for a ten-year-old. I wonder where they
went. Away with short trousers and pimples and everything else
I grew out of, of course.

Three boys of about twelve were crowded around a pinball
machine. As they moved apart momentarily he saw that they
were trying to start it with a coin on a piece of wire. He took a
stride towards them and opened his mouth—but suppose they
turned on him? If they set about him, pulled him down and
kicked him, his shouts would never be heard for the uproar.

There was no sign of an attendant. Stone hurried back to
the merry-go-round, where several little girls were mounting
horses. "Those boys are up to no good," he complained to the
man in the frame.

"You! Yes, you! I've seen you before. Don't let me see you
again," the man shouted. They dispersed, swaggering.

"Things didn't use to be like this," Stone said, breathing
hard with relief. "I suppose your merry-go-round is all that's left
of the old fairground."

"The old one? No, this didn't come from there."

"I thought the old one must have been taken over."

"No, it's still there, what's left of it," the man said. "I don't
know what you'd find there now. Through that exit is the quick-
est way. You'll come to the side entrance in five minutes, if it's
still open."

The moon had risen. It glided along the rooftops as Stone
emerged from the back of the funfair and hurried along the

terraced street. Its light lingered on the tips of chimneys and the peaks of roofs. Inside the houses, above slivers of earth or stone that passed for front gardens, Stone saw faces silvered by television.

At the end of the terrace, beyond a wider road, he saw an identical street paralleled by an alley. Just keep going. The moon cleared the roofs as he crossed the intersection, and left a whitish patch on his vision. He was trying to blink it away as he reached the street, and so he wasn't certain if he glimpsed a group of boys emerging from the street he'd just left and running into the alley.

Anxiety hurried him onwards while he wondered if he should turn back. His car was on the promenade; he could reach it in five minutes. They must be the boys he had seen in the pin-ball arcade, out for revenge. Quite possibly they had knives or broken bottles; no doubt they knew how to use them from the television. His heels clacked in the silence. Dark exits from the alley gaped between the houses. He tried to set his feet down gently as he ran. The boys were making no sound at all, at least none that reached him. If they managed to overbalance him they could smash his bones while he struggled to rise. At his age that could be worse than dangerous. Another exit lurked between the houses, which looked threatening in their weight and impassivity. He must stay on his feet whatever happened. If the boys got hold of his arms he could only shout for help. The houses fell back as the street curved, their opposite numbers loomed closer. In front of him, beyond a wall of corrugated tin, lay the old fairground.

He halted panting, trying to quell his breath before it blotted out any sounds in the alley. Where he had hoped to find a well-lit road to the promenade, both sides of the street ended as if lopped, and the way was blocked by the wall of tin. In the middle, however, the tin had been prised back like a lid, and a jagged entrance yawned among the sharp shadows and moonlit inscriptions. The fairground was closed and deserted.

As he realised that the last exit was back beyond the curve of the street, Stone stepped through the gap in the tin. He stared down the street, which was empty but for scattered fragments of brick and glass. It occurred to him that they might not have been the same boys after all. He pulled the tin to, behind him, and looked around.

The circular booths, the long target galleries, the low roller coaster, the ark and the crazy house draped shadow over each other and merged with the dimness of the paths between. Even the merry-go-round was hooded by darkness hanging from its canopy. Such wood as he could see in the moonlight looked ragged, the paint patchy. But between the silent machines and stalls one ride was faintly illuminated: the Ghost Train.

He walked towards it. Its front was emitting a pale green glow which at first sight looked like moonlight, but which was brighter than the white tinge the moon imparted to the adjoining rides. Stone could see one car on the rails, close to the entrance to the ride. As he approached, he glimpsed from the corner of his eye a group of men, stallholders presumably, talking and gesticulating in the shadows between two stalls. So the fairground wasn't entirely deserted. They might be about to close, but perhaps they would allow him one ride, seeing that the Ghost Train was still lit. He hoped they hadn't seen him using the vandals' entrance.

As he reached the ride and realised that the glow came from a coat of luminous paint, liberally applied but now rather dull and threadbare, he heard a loud clang from the tin wall. It might have been someone throwing a brick, or someone reopening the torn door; the stalls obstructed his view. He glanced quickly about for another exit, but found none. He might run into a dead end. It was best to stay where he was. He couldn't trust the stallholders; they might live nearby; they might know the boys or even be their parents. As a child he'd once run to someone who had proved to be his attacker's unhelpful father. He climbed into the Ghost Train car.

Nothing happened. Nobody was attending the ride. Stone strained his ears. Neither the boys, if they were there, nor the attendant seemed to be approaching. If he called out the boys would hear him. Instead, frustrated and furious, he began to kick the metal inside the nose of the car.

Immediately the car trundled forward over the lip of an incline in the track and plunged through the Ghost Train doors into darkness.

As he swung 'round an unseen clattering curve, surrounded by noise and the dark, Stone felt as if he had suddenly become the victim of delirium. He remembered his storm-racked childhood bed and the teeming darkness pouring into him. Why on earth had he come on this ride? He'd never liked ghost trains as a child, and as he grew up he had instinctively avoided them. He'd allowed his panic to trap him. The boys might be waiting when he emerged. Well, in that case he would appeal to whoever was operating the ride. He sat back, gripping the wooden seat beneath him with both hands, and gave himself up to the straining of metal, the abrupt swoops of the car, and the darkness.

Then, as his anxiety about the outcome of the ride diminished, another impression began to trickle back. As the car had swung around the first curve he'd glimpsed an illuminated shape, two illuminated shapes, withdrawn so swiftly that he'd had no time to glance up at them. He had the impression that they had been the faces of a man and a woman, gazing down at him. At once they had vanished into the darkness or been swept away by it. It seemed to him for some reason very important to remember their expressions.

Before he could pursue this, he saw a greyish glow ahead of him. He felt an unreasoning hope that it would be a window, which might give him an idea of the extent of the darkness. But already he could see that its shape was too irregular. A little closer and he could make it out. It was a large stuffed grey rabbit with huge glass or plastic eyes, squatting upright in an alcove with its front paws extended before it. Not a dead rabbit, of course: a toy. Beneath him the car was clattering and shaking, yet he had the odd notion that this was a deliberate effect, that in fact the car had halted and the rabbit was approaching or growing. Rubbish, he thought. It was a pretty feeble ghost, anyway. Childish. His hands pulled at splinters on the wooden seat beneath him. The rabbit rushed towards him as the track descended a slight slope. One of its eyes was loose, and whitish stuffing hung down its cheek from the hole. The rabbit was at least four feet tall. As the car almost collided with it before whipping away around a curve, the rabbit toppled towards him and the light that illuminated it went out.

Stone gasped and clutched his chest. He'd twisted 'round to look behind him at the darkness where he judged the rabbit to have been, until a spasm wrenched him frontward again. Light tickling drifted over his face. He shuddered, then relaxed. Of course they always had threads hanging down for cobwebs, his friends had told him that. But no wonder the fairground was deserted, if this was the best they could do. Giant toys lit up, indeed. Not only cheap but liable to give children nightmares.

The car coursed up a slight incline and down again before shaking itself in a frenzy around several curves. Trying to soften you up before the next shock, Stone thought. Not me, thank you very much. He lay back in his seat and sighed loudly with boredom. The sound hung on his ears like muffs. Why did I do that? he wondered. It's not as if the operator can hear me. Then who can?

Having spent its energy on the curves, the car was slowing. Stone peered ahead, trying to anticipate. Obviously he was meant to relax before the car startled him with a sudden jerk. As he peered, he found his eyes were adjusting to the darkness. At least he could make out a few feet ahead, at the side of the track, a squat and bulky grey shape. He squinted as the car coasted towards it. It was a large armchair.

The car came abreast of it and halted. Stone peered at the chair. In the dim hectic flecked light, which seemed to attract and outline all the restless discs on his eyes, the chair somehow looked larger than he. Perhaps it was farther away than he'd thought. Some clothes thrown over the back of the chair looked diminished by it, but they could be a child's clothes. If nothing else, Stone thought, it's instructive to watch my mind working. Now let's get on.

Then he noticed that the almost invisible light was flickering. Either that, which was possible although he couldn't determine the source of the light, or the clothes were shifting; very gradually but nonetheless definitely, as if something hidden by them was lifting them to peer out, perhaps preparatory to emerging. Stone leaned towards the chair. Let's see what it is, let's get it over with. But the light was far too dim, the chair too distant. Probably he would be unable to see it even when it emerged, the way the light had been allowed to run down, unless he left the car and went closer.

He had one hand on the side of the car when he realised that if the car moved off while he was out of it he would be left to grope his way through the darkness. He slumped back, and as he did so he glimpsed a violent movement among the clothes near the seat of the chair. He glanced towards it. Before his eyes could focus, the dim grey light was extinguished.

Stone sat for a moment, all of him concentrating on the silence, the blind darkness. Then he began to kick frantically at the nose of the car. The car shook a little with his attack, but stayed where it was. By the time it decided to move forward, the pressure of his blood seemed to be turning the darkness red.

When the car nosed its way around the next curve, slowing as if sniffing the track ahead, Stone heard a muted thud and creak of wood above the noise of the wheels. It came from in front of him. The sort of thing you hear in a house at night, he thought. Soon be out now.

Without warning a face came rushing towards him out of the darkness a few feet ahead. It jerked forward as he did. Of course it would, he thought with a grimace, sinking back and watching his face sink briefly into the mirror. Now he could see that he and the car were surrounded by a faint light that extended as far as the wooden frame of the mirror. Must be the end of the ride. They can't get any more obvious than that. Effective in its way, I suppose.

He watched himself in the mirror as the car followed the curve past. His silhouette loomed on the greyish light, which had fallen behind. Suddenly he frowned. His silhouette was moving independent of the movement of the car. It was beginning to swing out of the limits of the mirror. Then he remembered the wardrobe that had stood at the foot of his childhood bed, and realised what was happening. The mirror was set in a door, which was opening.

Stone pressed himself against the opposite side of the car, which had slowed almost to a halt. No no, he thought, it mustn't. Don't. He heard a grinding of gears beneath him; unmeshed metal shrieked. He threw his body forward, against the nose of the car. In the darkness to his left he heard the creak of the door and a soft thud. The car moved a little, then caught the gears and ground forward.

As the light went out behind him, Stone felt a weight fall beside him on the seat.

He cried out. Or tried to, for as he gulped in air it seemed to draw darkness into his lungs, darkness that swelled and poured into his heart and brain. There was a moment in which he knew nothing, as if he'd become darkness and silence and the memory of suffering. Then the car was rattling on, the darkness was sweeping over him and by, and the nose of the car banged open the doors and plunged out into the night.

As the car swung onto the length of track outside the Ghost Train, Stone caught sight of the gap between the stalls where he had thought he'd seen the stallholders. A welling moonlight showed him that between the stalls stood a pile of sacks, nodding and gesticulating in the wind. Then the seat beside him emerged from the shadow, and he looked down.

Next to him on the seat was a shrunken hooded figure. It wore a faded jacket and trousers striped and patched in various colours, indistinguishable in the receding moonlight. The head almost reached his shoulder. Its arms hung slack at its sides, and its feet drummed laxly on the metal beneath the seat. Shrinking away, Stone reached for the front of the car to pull himself to his feet, and the figure's head fell back.

Stone closed his eyes. When he opened them he saw within the hood an oval of white cloth upon which—black crosses for eyes, a barred crescent for a mouth—a grinning face was stitched.

As he had suddenly realised that the car hadn't halted nor even slowed before plunging down the incline back into the Ghost Train, Stone did not immediately notice that the figure had taken his hand.

THE TELL-TALE HEART

BY EDGAR ALLAN POE

TRUE!—NERVOUS—VERY, VERY DREADFULLY nervous I had been and am; but why will you say that I am mad? The disease had sharpened my senses—not destroyed—not dulled them. Above all was the sense of hearing acute. I heard all things in the heaven and in the earth. I heard many things in hell. How, then, am I mad? Hearken! and observe how healthily—how calmly I can tell you the whole story.

It is impossible to say how first the idea entered my brain; but once conceived, it haunted me day and night. Object there was none. Passion there was none. I loved the old man. He had never wronged me. He had never given me insult. For his gold I had no desire. I think it was his eye! Yes, it was this! He had the eye of a vulture—a pale blue eye, with a film over it. Whenever it fell upon me, my blood ran cold; and so by degrees—very gradually—I made up my mind to take the life of the old man, and thus rid myself of the eye forever.

Now this is the point. You fancy me mad. Madmen know nothing. But you should have seen me. You should have seen how wisely I proceeded—with what caution—with what foresight—with what dissimulation I went to work! I was never kinder to the old man than during the whole week before I killed him. And every night, about midnight, I turned the latch of his door and opened it—oh so gently! And then, when I had made an opening sufficient for my head, I put in a dark lantern, all closed, closed, that no light shone out, and then I thrust in my head. Oh, you would have laughed to see how cunningly I thrust it in! I moved it slowly—very, very slowly, so that I might not disturb the old man's sleep. It took me an hour to place my whole head within the opening so far that I could see him as he lay upon his bed. Ha! would a madman have been so wise as this? And then, when my head was well in the room, I undid the lantern cautiously—oh, so cautiously—cautiously (for the hinges creaked)—I undid it just so much that a single thin ray fell upon the vulture eye. And this I did for seven long nights—every night just at midnight—but I found the eye always closed; and so it was impossible to do the work; for it was not the old man who vexed me, but his Evil Eye. And every morning, when the day broke, I went boldly into the chamber, and spoke courageously to him, calling him by name in a hearty tone, and inquiring how he has passed the night. So you see he would have been a very profound old man, indeed, to suspect that every night, just at twelve, I looked in upon him while he slept.

Upon the eighth night I was more than usually cautious in opening the door. A watch's minute hand moves more quickly than did mine. Never before that night had I felt the extent of my own powers—of my sagacity. I could scarcely contain my feelings of triumph. To think that there I was, opening the door, little by little, and he not even to dream of my secret deeds or thoughts. I fairly chuckled at the idea; and perhaps he heard me; for he moved on the bed suddenly, as if startled. Now you may think that I drew back—but no. His room was as black as pitch with the thick darkness, (for the shutters were close fastened, through fear of robbers,) and so I knew that he could not see the opening of the door, and I kept pushing it on steadily, steadily.

I had my head in, and was about to open the lantern, when my thumb slipped upon the tin fastening, and the old man sprang up in bed, crying out—"Who's there?"

I kept quite still and said nothing. For a whole hour I did not move a muscle, and in the meantime I did not hear him lie down. He was still sitting up in the bed listening;—just as I have done, night after night, hearkening to the death watches in the wall.

Presently I heard a slight groan, and I knew it was the groan of mortal terror. It was not a groan of pain or of grief—oh, no!—it was the low stifled sound that arises from the bottom of the soul when overcharged with awe. I knew the sound well. Many a night, just at midnight, when all the world slept, it has welled up from my own bosom, deepening, with its dreadful echo, the terrors that distracted me. I say I knew it well. I knew what the old man felt, and pitied him, although I chuckled at heart. I knew that he had been lying awake ever since the first slight noise, when he had turned in the bed. His fears had been ever since growing upon him. He had been trying to fancy them causeless, but could not. He had been saying to himself—"It is nothing but the wind in the chimney—it is only a mouse crossing the floor," or "It is merely a cricket which has made a single chirp." Yes, he had been trying to comfort himself with these suppositions: but he had found all in vain. All in vain; because Death, in approaching him had stalked with his black shadow before him, and enveloped the victim. And it was the mournful influence of the unperceived shadow that caused him to feel—although he neither saw nor heard—to feel the presence of my head within the room.

When I had waited a long time, very patiently, without hearing him lie down, I resolved to open a little—a very, very little crevice in the lantern. So I opened it—you cannot imagine how stealthily, stealthily—until, at length a simple dim ray, like the thread of the spider, shot from out the crevice and fell full upon the vulture eye.

It was open—wide, wide open—and I grew furious as I gazed upon it. I saw it with perfect distinctness—all a dull blue, with a hideous veil over it that chilled the very marrow in my bones; but I could see nothing else of the old man's face or person: for I had directed the ray as if by instinct, precisely upon the damned spot.

And have I not told you that what you mistake for madness is but over-acuteness of the sense?—now, I say, there came to my ears a low, dull, quick sound, such as a watch makes when enveloped in cotton. I knew that sound well, too. It was the beating of the old man's heart. It increased my fury, as the beating of a drum stimulates the soldier into courage.

But even yet I refrained and kept still. I scarcely breathed. I held the lantern motionless. I tried how steadily I could maintain the ray upon the eve. Meantime the hellish tattoo of the heart increased. It grew quicker and quicker, and louder and louder every instant. The old man's terror must have been extreme! It grew louder, I say, louder every moment!—do you mark me well I have told you that I am nervous: so I am. And now at the dead hour of the night, amid the dreadful silence of that old house, so strange a noise as this excited me to uncontrollable terror. Yet, for some minutes longer I refrained and stood still. But the beating grew louder, louder! I thought the heart must burst. And now a new anxiety seized me—the sound would be heard by a neighbour! The old man's hour had come! With a loud yell, I threw open the lantern and leaped into the room. He shrieked once—once only. In an instant I dragged him to the floor, and pulled the heavy bed over him. I then smiled gaily, to find the deed so far done. But, for many minutes, the heart beat on with a muffled sound. This, however, did not vex me; it would not be heard through the wall. At length it ceased. The old man was dead. I removed the bed and examined the corpse. Yes, he was stone, stone dead. I placed my hand upon the heart and held it there many minutes. There was no pulsation. He was stone dead. His eve would trouble me no more.

If still you think me mad, you will think so no longer when I describe the wise precautions I took for the concealment of the body. The night waned, and I worked hastily, but in silence. First of all I dismembered the corpse. I cut off the head and the arms and the legs.

I then took up three planks from the flooring of the chamber, and deposited all between the scantlings. I then replaced the boards so cleverly, so cunningly, that no human eye—not even his—could have detected any thing wrong. There was nothing to wash out—no stain of any kind—no blood-spot whatever. I had been too wary for that. A tub had caught all—ha! ha!

When I had made an end of these labors, it was four o'clock—still dark as midnight. As the bell sounded the hour, there came a knocking at the street door. I went down to open it with a light heart,—for what had I now to fear? There entered three men, who introduced themselves, with perfect suavity, as officers of the police. A shriek had been heard by a neighbour during the night; suspicion of foul play had been aroused; information had been lodged at the police office, and they (the officers) had been deputed to search the premises.

I smiled,—for what had I to fear? I bade the gentlemen welcome. The shriek, I said, was my own in a dream. The old man, I mentioned, was absent in the country. I took my visitors all over the house. I bade them search—search well. I led them, at length, to his chamber. I showed them his treasures, secure, undisturbed. In the enthusiasm of my confidence, I brought chairs into the room, and desired them here to rest from their fatigues, while I myself, in the wild audacity of my perfect triumph, placed my own seat upon the very spot beneath which reposed the corpse of the victim.

The officers were satisfied. My manner had convinced them. I was singularly at ease. They sat, and while I answered cheerily, they chatted of familiar things. But, ere long, I felt myself getting pale and wished them gone. My head ached, and I fancied a ringing in my ears: but still they sat and still chatted. The ringing became more distinct:—It continued and became more distinct: I talked more freely to get rid of the feeling: but it continued and gained definiteness—until, at length, I found that the noise was not within my ears.

No doubt I now grew very pale;—but I talked more fluently, and with a heightened voice. Yet the sound increased—and what could I do? It was a low, dull, quick sound—much such a sound as a watch makes when enveloped in cotton. I gasped for breath—and yet the officers heard it not. I talked more quickly—more vehemently; but the noise steadily increased. I arose and argued about trifles, in a high key and with violent gesticulations; but the noise steadily increased. Why would they not be gone? I paced the floor to and fro with heavy strides, as if excited to fury by the observations of the men—but the noise steadily increased. Oh God! what could I do? I foamed—I raved—I swore! I swung the chair upon which I had been sitting, and grated it upon the boards, but the noise arose over all and continually increased. It grew louder—louder—louder! And still the men chatted pleasantly, and smiled. Was it possible they heard not? Almighty God!—no, no! They heard!—they suspected!—they knew!—they were making a mockery of my horror!—this I thought, and this I think. But anything was better than this agony! Anything was more tolerable than this derision! I could bear those hypocritical smiles no longer! I felt that I must scream or die! and now—again!—hark! louder! louder! louder! louder!

"Villains!" I shrieked, "dissemble no more! I admit the deed!—tear up the planks! here, here!—It is the beating of his hideous heart!"

A MOTHER'S LOVE

BRIAN JAMES FREEMAN

ANDREW STOPPED SHORT of where the hallways on the fourth floor of the Sunny Days Hospice Home crossed. Two nurses were gabbing around the corner and he didn't care for the people who worked here. The employees liked to chat with anyone they spotted, and at first he thought they were being friendly, but soon enough he realized they were just being nosy. Who were you here to see, what was your relationship, were you approved by the family—stupid, invasive questions.

His mother was alone right now, and Andrew hated when he wasn't by her side, but he was doing the best he could under the circumstances. He worked to pay their bills and keep their lives in some semblance of order as hers was coming to an end. He ran errands, buying her favorite cigarettes even after the doctor told her to drop the bad habit while she still could (as if that would make any difference at this late date), and he undertook any tasks that simply had to be done.

Once the nurses continued on their rounds, Andrew scurried along as quietly as he could, trying not to draw attention to himself. He remembered his first visit to this building, to a clean and well-lit office near the lobby where he begged the admissions lady, Miss Clarence, to please accept his mother into the facility, to please help him move her from his childhood home where he could no longer care for her properly.

Miss Clarence examined the paperwork Andrew completed in his thick block handwriting, and of course the first issue raised was whether he would have the money required, but he said he could cover the fees if they let him pay in installments until he could sell the house. That had to be possible, right?

It was, and Andrew felt relief wash over him, but then Miss Clarence surprised him with a bigger problem he hadn't anticipated: the lack of available beds at Sunny Days for new patients.

"What do you mean?" Andrew asked, his hands shaking. "Isn't everyone here dying?"

"Well, Mr. Smith," the young woman behind the desk patiently explained, "Our guests reside with us for as long as necessary to complete their life journey. We don't like to use the word *dying*. So final and crude. We like to say, they're *moving on*."

"But how long until a bed opens up?"

"There's no way to know for certain, but if you'll agree to the payment plan we discussed, we'll call you as soon as there's a room available. Do you understand, Mr. Smith?"

Andrew had understood all right. He would be spending his entire life savings and then some for his mother's short stay in this place, but the people in charge were going to make him wait for the privilege. Powerful people liked to make the little people wait to flaunt their control over you. Andrew knew this. His mother had taught him well.

But still, he signed the financial paperwork and went home. What other option was there? He loved his mother, and she loved him, and he would do whatever she needed him to do. He understood there was nothing in the world like a mother's love. No girlfriend, no wife, not even another member of your family could love you the way your mother loved you, and you had to love her back just as much, maybe more.

Now Andrew was consumed by a different kind of waiting. The time of his mother's death—her *moving on*, to use Miss Clarence's term—was drawing nearer. He loved his mother so much and he needed to be there when her last moments on Earth came to pass. Being with his mother as she died, to keep her from being alone, was his responsibility.

Andrew walked down the bright and cheerful hallway, wincing whenever his shoes squeaked on the gleaming buffed floor. A television blared *Jeopardy* from somewhere, but many of the rooms were silent. The almost-dead didn't make much noise.

He neared the last doorway on the right, where the hallway terminated with a window overlooking a grove of trees. The sun was setting beyond the mountains in the distance and the sky blazed red and orange and shades of purple as if the air had caught fire.

Andrew stopped outside the door.

Could he really do what he had come here to do?

After all of these years of being his mother's only son, her best friend in the entire world, and the only person who loved her as much as she loved him, could he *really* do what needed to be done?

He had to, of course, he just had to, but self-doubt weighed heavily on his heart. He had decided on the way here that the best approach would be to think as little as possible once he was in the room. Forget emotions, forget humanity, forget the rules of nature, and become like a machine for a few minutes. Be cold, follow through, and then go home and force himself to forget his actions as soon as possible.

Andrew opened the door with those thoughts looping in his mind. The fiery sky bled in through the window and washed across the hospital-style bed where the old woman slept. Her skin was wrinkled and her teeth were yellowed. Her withered chest rose and fell. He leaned in to hear her wheezing. He could smell the cigarettes on her breath. The familiar stench was unmistakable.

Andrew stood motionless, just watching, and he realized he had to move or he would lose his nerve.

He put one shaking hand across her dry mouth. She snorted. He froze again.

Be cold, Andrew told himself, *be cold cold cold cold.*

He squeezed her nose closed with his index finger and a thumb. Her head tilted and her eyes blinked open. She was groggy and confused, and she rolled onto her side as if to get out of the bed, but he leaned forward to block her.

Reacting with surprising quickness, she reached up and clawed at his face with her brittle nails. The pain was intense. Blood trickled from his pierced skin. He hadn't planned on there being any blood; he hadn't expected her to wake up. He had assumed she would peacefully go to sleep forever.

Andrew doubled the pressure with his hand and fingers, turning his head away and closing his eyes to avoid her wild, perplexed, angry gaze.

Her torso bucked and she swatted at the back of his head with those calloused and bony fingers. There was so much life bursting from inside her in her final moments!

Then her body stilled, her jaw slackened, and the fight seemed to empty out of her as quickly as it had arrived.

She was silent.

Andrew kept his eyes closed as tears welled up. He had done it. He had really done it.

He slipped out of the room and hurried home.

When Andrew entered the tiny house where he had lived his entire life, he didn't bother turning on the lights.

A Mother's Love

How many times had he walked that hallway at Sunny Days, planning what he would do and then chickening out? How would his life change now that he had finally gone through with it? And how would he deal with a memory he knew would haunt him until his own death?

Andrew sat at the kitchen table and waited for the phone call. He would need to act surprised at the news. He felt hollow inside, as if his mother's cancer had actually been eating away at him, too, but he was sure his mother would be proud of him. She had always loved him so much, and he had always tried to return her love twice over or even more, doing whatever she needed him to do, going above and beyond to make her happy and comfortable, especially as her health deteriorated and the end grew closer.

When the phone finally rang, Andrew answered with a meek, barely audible: "Hello?"

"Hello? Mr. Smith? This is Miss Clarence from Sunny Days Hospice Home."

"Yes, Miss Clarence?"

"I'm glad I could reach you personally, Mr. Smith. One of our guests has moved on and we have a bed ready for your mother."

"Well, that's just swell," Andrew said, barely feeling like himself. "I'll go tell her."

He hung up the phone and made his way to the bedroom where his mother slept, where she had spent the last six months while her body weakened and death patiently waited for her to give up the fight.

Andrew loved his mother so much and he was relieved to finally have some good news to share with her.

THE KEEPER'S COMPANION

JOHN AJVIDE LINDQVIST

1

ALBERT WAS BORN to be a game master. Even when he was a little boy he was the one who guided his friends through fantasy worlds where they hunted for treasure and battled against monsters. He had the authority, he had the imagination. And he had the language.

His mother was a comparatively well-known writer of children's books, and his father taught Swedish at high school. As long as Albert could remember he had been part of an ongoing conversation where his views were taken seriously. He was able to read and write by the time he started school, and he had a vocabulary not far behind that of his teacher.

During both elementary school and junior high he positively devoured books, mainly fantasy and horror. Sport had never interested him, and he had only a small number of friends. So he read. He played on his Xbox too, but it wasn't really his thing, so to speak. Over the years a vague feeling of dissatisfaction began to grow within him, as if there were something to be achieved, something he couldn't quite put his finger on.

He was twelve years old when he was introduced to the role playing game Dungeons and Dragons, and suddenly he knew exactly where to put that finger. The books accompanying the game contained knowledge that could be used even though it wasn't factual: detailed maps of an imaginary continent, produced purely for the purposes of the game.

When Albert became a game master after several weeks of preparation, it was as if pieces of himself that had lain strewn around unused since his childhood finally fell into place. Sitting at the head of the table he verbally conjured up the dangers and pleasures, the characters and monsters of The forgotten realms, while the three boys with whom he was playing sat spellbound. Albert knew: this was his thing. The authority, the imagination, the language. This was what he was born for.

Albert had never been popular in school, but he had never been bullied either. He had two friends, Tore and Wille; admittedly their classmates called them geeks when they quoted lines from The Lord of the Rings, but that was as bad as it got.

The dark energy of the class was principally directed towards Oswald, a spotty, podgy boy who didn't smell too good, on top of everything else. In fact, he was the one who was closest to Albert in terms of his linguistic and educational ability, but hanging out with Oswald was the mark of a loser, so when Oswald became a target, Albert wasn't slow to join in. He had the facility to come up with nicknames that stuck; for example, he was the one who decided to call Oswald the Whoopee Cushion in a nod to the boy's bulk and the unpleasant odor that surrounded him. It was an epithet that Oswald carried for years.

Albert had a high opinion of himself. He knew that he was more intelligent than most of his peers, better able to express himself, and that through his intellect he could gain power over others. Someone like Oswald had nothing in his locker to match Albert.

And yet it was Oswald who initiated the next leap forward in Albert's development. By this time, they were fourteen years old and in eighth grade. Oswald had lost some weight and didn't smell quite so bad. He was still called the Whoopee Cushion, of course, but he and Albert did chat occasionally, because after all they shared the same literary interests.

It was during one of these conversations that Oswald hauled out the book he was currently reading: Necronomicon—The Best Weird Tales of H.P. Lovecraft. It was the size and weight of a doorstop. Albert knew enough to be able to fake a deeper proficiency. He flicked idly through the thick volume while Oswald enthused over the dark universe Lovecraft had created, and the enormous amount of literature surrounding it.

That same evening Albert asked his father to order the book for him from Amazon. All his life things had been the same: if Albert wanted a book, he got it. While he was waiting for his new acquisition to arrive, he looked up Lovecraft on the internet and eventually discovered Chaosium and the role playing game Call of Cthulhu. After a few hours' surfing Albert's father was asked to supplement his order with the basic rule book, plus the accompanying paperback The Keeper's Companion. His parents had always encouraged Albert's role playing too.

One Friday evening in February Albert was the Keeper as the Game Master was called in CoC for "The Haunting", a beginner's adventure from the rule book. As usual he and three friends had gathered in the cellar of Albert's house, which had been set up as a hobby room with a table tennis table, a work-bench and a big dining table, perfect for just such an occasion. Tore and Wille were there, plus Linus, a boy from another class who often wore a T-shirt with the slogan "Winter is coming".

The characters were introduced and their background stories invented, then Albert led the others through the investigation of Mr Corbitt's haunted house. He outlined the rumors that were circulating, played the various people they came across, built up the atmosphere. The dampness, the darkness, the smell of mold in the old house.

Call of Cthulhu had something that was lacking in Dungeons and Dragons: suggestion. Okay, there was a certain amount of tension as you prepared to enter a cave where you knew a monster was hiding, but this was something else. The pattern of the game, the whole world where insanity constantly lurked, seemed to have been designed to create the perception of an underlying threat, of terrifying suspicions. They had been playing for several hours and were just about to go down into Mr Corbitt's cellar when Albert's mother tapped on the door. All four of them leapt in the air and let out a scream. That was when Albert really began to love Call of Cthulhu.

When it was all over one character was dead and another was in the lunatic asylum. It was five o'clock in the morning, the boys had consumed twelve cans of Celsius energy drink and couldn't stop talking about how fucking fantastic it had been. The atmosphere was one of exhausted euphoria, and if they had been a little younger they might have raced out into the forest to do some live role play in order to work off an excess of emotion. Instead they talked. Talked and talked until the sun came up and Albert's three friends staggered homewards. Dungeons and Dragons had been the thing, yes, but this was the thing!

As the months went by rumors spread about the unbelievable game playing experiences in Albert's cellar. Linus in particular couldn't help boasting about their adventures. Things went so far that the two toughest boys in the class and the second-prettiest girl made a tentative approach: could they come along some time?

No, they couldn't. Six players was far too many to maintain the atmosphere, so Albert made an investment for the future. Instead of the usual group, he invited the two boys and the girl one Friday evening and reprised "The Haunting". Since he had already led the adventure once, he was able to fine tune the details.

The three of them were nowhere near as good as Tore, Wille and Linus when it came to playing the game; they didn't have the same breadth of imagination, and weren't as adept at remaining in tune with their characters, but they couldn't help being gripped by the power of suggestion. Daniel, who competed in MMA and had once given Albert a wedgie back in sixth grade, sat there wide-eyed and open-mouthed drinking in every word that fell from his lips. When it was time to go down into Mr Corbitt's cellar, Olivia was so scared that she started to cry.

They left Albert's house at around four in the morning, all in agreement that this was one of the most fantastic things they'd ever experienced. A successful investment, one could say.

It would be an exaggeration to say that Albert became king after this, but his status was certainly boosted. A games evening round at Albert's was highly desirable, and he made a point of arranging sessions for the less initiated occasionally, just to keep his reputation alive.

Oswald kept asking if he could come along, but Albert said no. By this time he had suppressed the fact that it was Oswald who had introduced him to Lovecraft, and he saw no reason to waste his talents on someone who would actually lower his status. Besides which Oswald had a deeper understanding than anyone else, including Albert.

Albert had forbidden Wille, Tore and Linus from reading Lovecraft. The characters in the game didn't know what they were battling against, and therefore the players shouldn't know either. The idea of Oswald, with his encyclopedic knowledge, playing the role of a completely uninformed individual just wouldn't work, and Albert told him so. What he didn't tell Oswald was that he was afraid of having his authority challenged. He did, however, mention the odor surrounding Oswald.

During the summer vacation Albert tackled something he had been planning for a long time, but as a conscientious student he hadn't had the time: he wanted to create his own adventure. With his three core players he had worked through Spawn of Tsathogghua, The Fungi from Yuggoth and half of Masks of Nyarlathotep, but now he was going to create his own world within the Cthulhu universe, preferably something located in Stockholm.

Albert began to build a narrative centered on the construction of Stockholm's City Library, a room containing forbidden books where Ludwig Prinn's De Vermis Mysteriis was the principal treasure, an unpleasant cult led by the library's architect Gunnar Asplund, and a crescendo that would coincide with the inauguration of the library in 1928.

He searched the internet for pictures of the city around that time, studied the tram routes, the role of the police, smuggling, and the political situation. When he started ninth grade in the middle of August, he had created an adventure that, in his opinion, was as good as anything Sandy Petersen had come up with, and he had ambitious plans to translate it into English himself and sell it to Chaosium. He had thought of a title—The Lurker in the Library—but found it was taken, and had to settle for the less catchy The Shambler of Stockholm.

As the time to play the adventure grew nearer, Albert was once again approached by Oswald, and in the end it was Albert's vanity that made him give in. He had created his own world with laws that to a certain extent deviated from the conventional and would therefore be unfamiliar to Oswald, but in many ways the norm still applied in a way that made sense. Oswald was the only one with the knowledge that would enable him to fully appreciate Albert's achievement, so Albert said "Okay".

"Okay what?" Oswald asked, with a look on his face not unlike that of a dog whose master has just reached for a box of treats.

"Okay, you can play."

The dog analogy became even more appropriate when Oswald began to tremble, and appeared to be dribbling with excitement when he opened his mouth. Before Oswald could spray him with saliva, Albert held up his hand. "Once. On a trial basis. Then we'll see."

Oswald nodded eagerly, assuring Albert that he wouldn't show off, but would be a complete ignoramus. "What was it called again?" he asked. "Catullu?"

Albert smiled graciously and told him to be there on Friday at seven.

The rest of the gang weren't happy about Oswald's inclusion. They had gone from puberty to raging hormones, and Linus's T-shirt now bore a picture of Tyrion Lannister and the words "I am the god of tits and wine". Oswald's presence was like having an out-sider observing their game, which was possibly way too childish.

However, all their reservations were blown away when they began to play. Albert's narrative worked beautifully, and Oswald's character was soon an indispensable part of the group. He was an arms expert who could read and write Latin, and the adventure involved confrontations with armed hench-men, and a number of texts in Latin. Oswald also managed not to show off, just as he'd promised. Admittedly the corners of his mouth could be seen twitching when Albert talked about Ludwig Prinn, but he said nothing.

And there was no denying it: Oswald was an exemplary player, one hundred per cent attentive to everything Albert said, and so receptive to suggestion that his lips trembled when the situation became particularly critical. He also offered plenty of ideas, and was incredibly lucky with the dice.

They stopped at four o'clock in the morning, having reached a natural break in the story. As usual, the atmosphere was one of high excitement. De Vermis Mysteriis was within reach, and once they had acquired it the next phase would begin. They decided to resume playing the very next evening. As they were about to leave, Albert said: "Okay, see you tomorrow".

Wille, Tore and Linus were on their way out, but Oswald didn't move. His self-confidence had grown over the course of the evening, but now his inner lapdog reappeared as he quietly asked: "Does that include me?" Before Albert had time to respond, Wille said: "What are you talking about? That fucking book's in Latin—we need you."

Albert wasn't pleased to see Wille usurping his authority. He was the game master, this was his house and his adventure; it wasn't Wille's place to invite people along. Fortunately for Oswald, he realized this. He smiled wanly at Wille, then turned his pleading doggy eyes to Albert, who nodded and said: "Of course, Oswald. See you tomorrow".

Oswald's expression suggested that he would have liked to jump on Albert and give his face a good licking.

When Albert woke up in the afternoon, he shoveled down a bowl of muesli with yogurt before preparing the evening's activities. His mother and father were on a weekend break in Paris, so the group had the house to themselves. The others were supplying pizza; there had to be some privileges when you were the game master.

If the players followed the dramatic curve that Albert had planned, a climax should be reached when they entered the underground chamber in the library where De Vermis Mysteriis was kept. Unfortunately Gunnar Asplund himself was in there too, protected by a Barrier of Naach-Tith, from which he would read a spell that summoned a star vampire.

The problem lay in finding the right details so that something magnificent and horrific didn't become inane. Albert began by rereading Robert Bloch's short story The Shambler from the Stars, where the star vampire is mentioned for the first time. The eerie giggling emanating from the invisible creature, its appearance when it has drunk the blood of its victim and its contours begin to emerge. The formless, pulsating mass. The tentacles.

One sticking point was the spell, the one the characters would hear as they stood listening outside the closed door. Albert had started with the one in the story: "Signa stellarum nigrarum et bufaniformis..." and had added a number of invocations from The Keeper's Companion: "Ia Shub-Niggurath, y'ai'ng'ngah, yog-sothoth", along with odd fragments along the lines of: "Ph'nglui mglw'nafh Cthulhu R'lyeh wgah'nagl fhtagn!" He repeated his invocation in order to make the words flow, and to ensure that he sounded as sinister as possible.

He had one specific goal: to make Oswald cry. He had come close a couple of times the previous evening; Oswald's eyes had been suspiciously shiny. But tonight those tears were definitely going to fall.

The evening came, the pizzas were eaten and the game began. As an extra touch, Albert had brought down a pair of candelabras so that they could play by the glow of candlelight. The dice rattled across the table and the tension grew in direct proportion to the number of cans of Celsius the boys consumed. By midnight the characters were finally standing outside the closed door at the bottom of the long staircase.

Albert had carefully built up the atmosphere, describing the vibrations in the stone walls, the smell of the prehistoric bog rising from the underworld, the beam of the flashlight which seemed to be swallowed up by the compact darkness, the sound of the blasphemous invocation. He lowered his voice, making the pitch as deep as possible, and began to intone: "Ph'nglui mglw'nafh Cthulhu R'lyeh wgah'nagl fhtagn ny'ar rot hotep..."

He could feel the quivering energy spreading through the room as the players realized they were facing something that could possibly kill them all. Albert glanced at Oswald, whose gaze was fixed on Albert's lips while he subconsciously moved his own lips. There were tears in his eyes.

Go on, cry, you pathetic worm.

Albert raised his voice a fraction and intensified the spell. He had abandoned his written text and started to improvise. The words just seemed to come to him, and he spat them out with a malicious potency he hadn't known he was capable of. And there it was, a tear trickling down Oswald's cheek as his lips continued to move in time with Albert's. It felt good to have another person's emotions in the palm of his hand; Albert could do whatever he wanted with them. He flung his arms wide and was about to declaim a final "Ia! Ia'y!" when something happened to the room.

Albert felt dizzy as the planes and angles altered. Corners became sharp edges, and the sides of the table folded in on themselves, causing Albert to lose his balance. He fell forward, his field of vision contracting until he could see only the six candle flames flickering at the end of a tunnel. In a way that was impossible to describe he knew that the flames were holding up the sticks of wax and not vice versa.

A second, and then it was over. By the time his forehead hit the table it was once again a solid surface made of birch, and behind a red curtain he heard his friends calling out: "Albie, what the fuck?" "What happened?" "What are you doing?" He got to his feet, staggered slightly and rubbed his head.

What was that?

In spite of his perception of the collapsing room, it was the sight of the candles that had etched itself into his brain as an indisputable realization. Those white wax objects were an adjunct to and a consequence of the slender yellow flames rising from the wicks. Cause and effect had changed places in a way that made his head spin, and he covered his eyes with his hands as he heard Wille say: "For fuck's sake, Albie, this is creepy enough as it is—there's no need to go over the top".

Albert lowered his hands and opened his eyes. The room looked perfectly normal, and the four boys were sitting around the table staring at him. Faint traces of tears shimmered on Oswald's cheeks in the yellow glow of the candlelight.

The flame produces the wick, the light creates the fire.

The pain in Albert's skull subsided and he was himself once more. He opened his mouth to say something, smooth things over, but not a sound emerged. A shiver ran down his spine as he realized that something was sitting behind him, looking at him. He slowly turned around and peered into the dark corner where the workbench stood.

The thing that was looking at him was sitting right in front of the bench. Was it sitting? He didn't know, because it was invisible, but he could feel its presence, its attention totally focused on him.

"What are you doing? Pack it in, Albie." Tore was standing next to him, shaking his shoulder. "Albie!"

Albert would have liked to respond, shrug his shoulders or smile, but he was paralyzed by fear. He could feel the power and the hunger emanating from the thing in front of the work-bench, and knew that he could be dead in a second. Tore shook him again. Nothing happened. Albert managed to force his jaws apart just enough to whisper: "Can you see anything? Over there in the corner?"

He pointed with a shaking finger, but was rewarded with a guffaw. "Seriously, Albie, pack it in! Come on, let's get back to the game."

Continuing to play was impossible. Even if he couldn't see the thing keeping watch in the corner, there was no way he was going to turn his back on it. He said he wasn't well and they'd have to carry on some other time; he claimed he didn't feel too good after banging his head.

$$\underset{\displaystyle \diagdown\!\diagdown}{\diagup\!\diagup}$$

As the others got ready to leave, muttering discontentedly, Albert glanced over at the corner where the nameless thing still sat, then turned to Wille. "Listen, can I come and stay at yours?"

"You said you didn't feel well."

"No, but... can I?"

Albert thought he ran the same risk of going mad as the characters in the game if he was forced to spend the night alone in the house with... that. To his relief, Wille shrugged and said: "Okay, as long as you don't throw up all over me."

Wille lived three doors down, and he and Albert had been friends for as long as they could remember. If there was one person Albert could confide in, it was Wille. They had said goodbye to the others and set off when Wille suddenly stopped and said: "So what really happened back there?"

Albert glanced down the street where the others were heading for the subway station. No awareness of indifferent evil, no thirst for blood in the air. He would have liked to persuade himself that the whole thing had been some kind of auto-suggestion, but the insight into the nature of the candles was burnt into his brain. Nothing was as he had thought, the most basic truths were wrong.

"What if..." he began. "What if this whole Cthulhu thing... What if it's actually possible to summon up something? If you say the right words?"

Wille tilted his head on one side. "Mmm?"

"What if I... accidentally did that."

"What are you talking about?"

"When I said those words. When we were in the library. It was as if something... happened. And something came."

Wille didn't laugh, didn't tell Albert that he was pushing things too far. In fact he seemed to regard it as a theoretical problem, because he said: "Well yes, but... it's all made up, isn't it? I mean it's not as if it's based on authentic sources or anything."

"No, but..."

"But what?"

"What if it is?"

They carried on talking, but Albert didn't mention the creature sitting in the corner because he was becoming more and more convinced that it had been a figment of his overheated imagination. Something had happened, but perhaps it was just a vision, like when people saw the Virgin Mary or Elvis. A temporary short circuit, a momentary blackout where reality is distorted.

They each grabbed a beer from Wille's father's stash, then sat chatting on the balcony for an hour or so. Towards the end of the conversation they had turned their attention to books and movies and girls, and Albert was beginning to feel quite mellow. They said goodnight, and Albert went into the guest room and closed the door. He was about to unzip his jeans when he froze on the spot and stopped breathing.

The guest room was also used as a home office, and at the far end there was a bookcase crammed with files and folders of different colors. In front of the bookcase sat the creature. Was the creature. It had no perceptible body, except perhaps the colors were slightly paler behind it, but that could be his imagination. Essentially it was invisible. And it was looking at Albert.

He slowly let the air out of his lungs, pushed down the door handle and backed out of the room without taking his eyes off the area where the creature was located. His breathing was rapid and shallow as he closed the door and stood there on the landing.

I'm going mad.

How many times had he pretended to be sympathetic as he threw the dice to determine what kind of insanity or phobia a character should suffer after being confronted with something that the human mind was incapable of dealing with?

Now he was in exactly the same position, and found that incipient madness did not take the form of hallucinatory images or a panic-stricken desire to flee; instead it was like a glutinous grey mass into which his consciousness was slowly sinking. His arms hanging limply by his side, he went downstairs, fighting the urge to stick out his tongue and let it dangle there.

He went into the living room and slumped down on the big sofa with its plumped up cushions a few feet away from the fifty-five-inch flat screen TV. He felt nothing, his thoughts were incapable of moving through the jelly-like fog that filled his head as he sat there staring at the black rectangle. He didn't even know when it happened, but at some point the creature materialized on the floor in front of the TV. It was looking at him. Waiting.

Terror had a stranglehold on Albert's throat, reducing it to what felt like the diameter of a straw, and the words came out as a broken whisper when he said: "What... do you want?"

No response. No change in the creature's focus, but in the silence of the room Albert thought he could hear something that sounded as if it came from far, far away, brushing against his eardrums through the ether. A joyless giggling.

Any attempt to get away would be futile. Albert stayed where he was on the sofa, staring at the thing that could not be seen, listening to the giggling that could not be heard. After about an hour he pulled a blanket over himself and curled up. There was a star vampire on the floor ten feet away from him.

De Vermis Mysteriis and Ludwig Prinn were creations of Robert Bloch, just like the creature itself. The incantations Albert had recited were a hotchpotch of Latin nonsense and Lovecraft's made-up language, which was based on Arabic.

And yet.

There were only two possibilities. The first was that he, Albert Egelsjö, a fifteen-year-old with a high IQ, no childhood trauma and a good relationship with his mother and father, had lost his mind. Started imagining things with such authenticity that they seemed real to him. He would end up in a child psych unit, with a diagnosis involving a whole series of capital letters, followed by a course of medication.

The other possibility was that a chain of coincidences had led him to cast a real spell, just as an infinite number of monkeys sitting at an infinite number of typewriters will eventually produce a Shakespeare play. That there was a real basis for

Lovecraft's universe, and that he had somehow made contact with it.

If he accepted that possibility, why didn't the creature attack him? It would be the work of a moment for the vampire to suck him dry before returning to the stars, giggling and sated with blood. Why was it just sitting there waiting?

Because...

The realization that flooded Albert's body made him sit bolt upright. It was obvious! It was only fear of the impossible that had prevented him from understanding; after all, he had been the game master in similar situations so many times.

In his adventure, Gunnar Asplund was in the secret library gabbling his spells. Not with the intention of summoning something that would suck the life out of him and cast him aside like an empty shell, oh no. His aim was to call up the creature because he needed its services. If the reality worked the same way as in the game, the creature was now bound to Albert until he gave it a command, a task that it must carry out, then it would be free to return to the place from which it had come.

A smile crept over Albert's lips as he stood up and pointed at the invisible presence. "You're mine, aren't you?" he whispered. "You will do whatever I tell you to do."

No response. But for a moment Albert thought the soulless giggling grew a little louder.

2

DAWN HAD BROKEN by the time Albert fell asleep, only to be woken two hours later by Wille's parents asking if he would like some breakfast. The creature appeared in the corner between the sink and the stove, its muted giggling drowned out by the sounds of everyday life.

Albert was in a world of his own as he chewed on a slice of bread with cheese and jam. From time to time he glanced over at the corner. A command. Theoretically, Albert could instruct the creature to remove Wille's family from the surface of the earth right now. Theoretically. In a second the lazy Sunday breakfast would be transformed into a bloody massacre, if Albert uttered just a few words. Or would the power of the mind be enough?

The creature was connected to his thoughts on the same wavelength as he himself was aware of its existence, a secret flow that linked the two of them. It was with some difficulty that Albert managed to swallow the lumps of masticated bread.

Wille's mother Veronica got to her feet, picked up her plate and walked over to the relevant area. Albert stiffened. What if someone touched the creature? Veronica stood by the sink, one leg within the presence.

Was Albert imagining the whole thing after all? Veronica was standing there rinsing her plate under the faucet and humming "Strangers in the Night" with one leg enveloped in a star vampire's shapeless mass. Did that seem like something that could actually happen?

Wille coughed loudly, and Albert turned away from the non-drama. Wille gave him a filthy look, and Albert stared uncomprehendingly back at him. Then he got it. He and Wille had once talked about older girls, well, women really, and Albert had mentioned that he thought Wille's mom was really hot. He might not have used that particular word, and he definitely hadn't gone as far as MILF, but Wille had reacted badly. His face had clouded over and he had changed the subject immediately.

And now Albert had spent quite some time sitting at the kitchen table staring at the lower half of Veronica's body; no doubt Wille thought he knew exactly what was going through Albert's mind. Fortunately, Wille's father Thomas was preoccupied with the morning paper, and didn't notice a thing.

Albert said thank you for breakfast, then got up from the table without taking his plate over to the sink as he usually did. He went into the hallway to put on his shoes; Wille followed him, his hands pushed deep into his pockets.

"What the fuck was that all about? You can't just fucking sit there eyeing up my mother like some kind of..."

"That wasn't what I was doing. Sorry, but it really wasn't."

"Okay... So what was it, then?"

"Can't you feel a... presence?"

"Not as far as you're concerned. Anything but, in fact."

Albert sighed. He wasn't going to get confirmation from Wille, yet he felt he had to carry on. "In the kitchen. Just now. It was exactly where your mom was standing. That's what I was looking at."

Wille nodded, his expression serious. "I get it. And now it's told you to go home and jerk off, right?"

"Fuck off."

'No, you fuck off."

※

Albert left Wille's house and strode down the garden path. He simply had to accept the facts. No one but him could see or perceive the extra-terrestrial visitor, and he was just going to have to deal with that.

It was a beautiful August morning, and the sun was already pleasantly warm as it shone down on the little gardens and fruit trees of Södra Ängby, with the sound of lawnmowers all around. It was as far from Lovecraft's fetid, gloomy world as it was possible to get.

And yet the visitor was fifteen feet away from Albert, next to the low fence surrounding the Ingessons' yard, closely observing his every movement. It was time to make a decision.

Was Albert capable of summoning up cosmic horrors, or was he soft in the head? He had no verifiable evidence to go on, so ultimately it was a question of faith. He examined the area of the sidewalk in which the creature was located and tried to think it away, to see only the paving stones and the Ingessons' white, slightly flaking fence, tried to convince himself that the silent presence was a mere figment of his imagination.

It was impossible. In spite of its lack of physicality, the visitor was as present as the sun up in the sky. There was nothing Albert could do about it, and he thought he was more likely to go insane if he denied it. The creature existed, however ethereal it might be. From now on, Albert would act accordingly. His feet began to move. Heading for home.

During the days that followed Albert tried to adapt to the new situation. The visitor was constantly by his side. It kept its vigil over him as he slept at night, and it was there when he got up in the mornings. Out on the street he was aware of its drifting, hovering presence, and when he entered a room it wasn't many seconds before he felt it watching him from a corner. Sometimes he would close his eyes, smack himself on the head or hum loudly just to avoid hearing that giggle, but to no avail. As soon as he fell silent and opened his eyes, he instantly knew that he was being observed and he could hear that sound, which seemed to come from something that was expectantly awaiting the outcome of a grotesque joke.

Just over a week after the creature came into Albert's life his class was involved in a volleyball tournament with a parallel group. Albert was useless when it came to anything involving a ball, and hardly anyone passed to him. The creature was sitting by the equipment store cupboard, following Albert's clumsy attempts to get the ball up in the air when it did occasionally come in his direction. This annoyed him. In some obscure way he wanted to be worthy of the visitor, but the ball slipped through his fingers as if they were made of smoke, and his team mates groaned.

He was in a foul mood in the shower afterwards, and it didn't help when Felix, a beefy idiot from the other class, started giving him grief. "Don't forget to wash your peanut-sized prick, Bilbo. If you can find it." Felix waggled his own penis, which was at least twice the size of Albert's.

Albert lowered his head and felt his cheeks redden. He was a thousand times cleverer than Felix and would probably be a success in life, while Felix would end up working for a removals firm or in some other dead-end job until he got fat on burgers and fries and drank himself to death.

Right now, however, they were next to one another in a scruffy, white-tiled shower room, and the only thing that counted was that Felix had more muscles and a bigger cock. Except for the creature's formless, malevolent presence emanating from the corner between the lockers and the toilet. It was watching Albert as he stood beneath the stream of water, with his head bent and his cheeks burning.

Felix twisted his towel a couple of times and whacked Albert across the backside. Albert only had to say the word, formulate the command in his mind. Tear him to pieces. Instead he grabbed his own towel and held it under the water until it was soaking wet. As Felix was on his way out of the room, Albert twisted his sodden towel into a hard sausage, then followed Felix and said: "Listen, asshole."

Felix spun around, the corners of his mouth turning up in a grimace that was a mixture of expectation and annoyance. Before he had time to do or say anything, Albert walloped the other boy's cock with the heavy toweling cosh. The corners of Felix's mouth turned down and he fell to his knees on the tiles, whimpering like a puppy. With every scrap of strength he could summon up, Albert brought the cosh down on his back. The sound of the blow bounced off the walls, and Felix shuddered.

"You need to keep your fucking mouth shut!" Albert yelled, twisting the wet towel even tighter. A thick, dark red weal appeared on Felix's back where the first blow had landed. Albert gathered his strength once more, all the way up from his toes; he swung the towel once more and brought it down in exactly the same place with such force that Felix fell forward and lay there on his stomach, shaking.

The skin above his hip had split, and a trickle of blood ran down onto the wet floor. Albert took aim once more and hit the wound so that it opened up, spattering his towel with blood. He dropped it, then bent down and picked up Felix's damp towel, which he used to dry himself. When he looked up he saw five or six boys standing in the doorway staring.

He wound Felix's towel around his hips. Now was the time to say something everyone would remember and repeat when they were sharing the story with friends or on social media, but his head was empty. Fortunately, Felix came to his assistance. With his cheek still glued to the tiles, he mumbled: "I'm going to... kill you... you fucking..."

Before Felix could come up with a suitable epithet, Albert interrupted him: "It might seem that way now. But when you think about it, insofar as you're capable of rational thought, you'll realize that's not a very good idea. You will be the one who dies, if you try anything. And that's a promise."

As Albert left the room he noticed that a couple of the boys had got out their phones. Hopefully only his final comment had been filmed.

That was indeed the case. The others had been too busy watching what was going on, and it had all happened so fast. However, Felix and Albert's final exchange was preserved for posterity to enjoy. In spite of the fact that the clip went viral among the students, it never came to the attention of any adult, and Felix wasn't the type to run crying to the principal. Nor did he make any attempt to carry out his threat to kill Albert.

Albert gave a great deal of thought to what had gone on. He had never used physical violence against anyone, nor did he have any desire to do so again. If he had felt that way, it would have been reasonable to suspect that the creature had driven him to act as he did, and was now aiming to ramp up the bloodshed. Stories like that did exist, after all, at least in the movies.

But Albert was pretty sure it wasn't about that. In the shower room the creature's only influence had consisted of its presence: it was there as a kind of guarantee, and Albert knew it. If Felix decided to jump him with a knife, Albert always had a way out. One word from his lips and the problem would be solved, without the slightest possibility that he could be suspected of having done what the creature was capable of.

Because he knew the creature now. During the time that had passed since he summoned it, he had felt a hint of a contact on a couple of occasions, and now and again—in a certain light, against a certain background—he had caught a glimpse of it.

It was more than a vampire, it was the embodiment of the very idea of a vampire, lacking all attributes except that which was needed to carry out its only task. To. Drain. Blood. The knowledge of its presence, always at the ready, gave Albert the courage to step beyond his previous limitations, as if he constantly had a loaded gun in his hand.

His old friends became less important to him, and role playing was something that belonged to the past. Albert changed. He had already had a high opinion of himself and his abilities, but now he acquired a physical stature that was in tune with his inner confidence. He started going to the gym. He had wanted to do it for a long time, but had been scared off by the bulging bodies working out behind the huge windows.

Now he had stopped apologizing for himself. The creature watched as Albert ploughed through a dozen pieces of equipment three times a week, but he hardly gave it a thought. The ripped guys were either pleasant towards him or ignored him completely.

At the end of October Albert got together with Olivia. A party, a kiss, a few text messages and phone calls, and then what had seemed unattainable became a reality. He had a girlfriend—not only that, she was the second hottest girl in the class. Wilma, who looked like a model, had never been seen with a boy, and to be honest that was unlikely to happen until Chris Hemsworth came knocking on the door. Or smashed it down with his hammer.

Having a girlfriend was fantastic. They talked, snuggled up on the sofa, watched films together; things went so far that Albert started sending emojis, something he had always regarded with the deepest contempt. But Olivia loved everything sweet, and once Albert had started, he just couldn't stop.

There was only one problem: the business of sex. Olivia had never been with anyone, so she wasn't exactly pushing, but once they had passed the stage of serious kissing and cuddling and dry humping there was a natural progression, to put it politely. You could only carry on slurping and squeezing for so long. Unfortunately, as soon as things got serious, when Olivia started taking off her clothes or undressing Albert, his cock went limp, and nothing helped.

He knew the reason, and it was also the reason why he had ended up lying in his bed helplessly caressing Olivia: the creature. He just couldn't do it with the creature sitting there watching him, couldn't perform in front of an audience, even if the audience was invisible and preternatural.

Albert made one excuse after another, but he could tell that Olivia was hurt. He might have begun to develop muscles, and following the incident with Felix no one dared give him a hard time, but what use was that if he was impotent? Sooner or later Olivia would talk to a friend, who would talk to another friend who would put something on Facebook, and that would be the end of that…

Besides which he wanted to do it, desperately. His groin was aching with lust, and his failure was giving him headaches. A week earlier Olivia had blushed as she confided that she was now on the pill, and if that wasn't an invitation, what was?

There was, of course, one obvious solution: he could simply say to the creature: "Go away and don't ever come back". However, for one thing he wasn't convinced that it would leave without slaking its thirst for blood, and for another… should he throw away a cosmic power factor just so that he could screw a girl? Sometimes he thought he should. More and more often, in fact.

What prevented him from acting was a lack of certainty about who he was without the creature. He was enjoying his status within the school, and didn't know if he would be able to maintain it without the creature's reassuring presence. Once you have acquired the taste for power over other people, it's hard to let it go.

⁂

One Friday evening when his parents had gone to the theatre to see some interminable play by Lars Norén, he invited Olivia 'round with the firm intention of doing it at long last. He had decanted a bottle of white wine from his parents' most recent wine box purchases, and he had bought prawns. It felt like such a cliché, but he didn't know what else to do.

He drank most of the wine himself to give him courage, and eventually his fingers stopped shaking enough to allow him to peel a couple of prawns and stuff them in his mouth. When they had cleared away they went to his room and lay down on the bed.

Albert had a very simple strategy. He turned off the light. He had already pulled down the blind, so the room was now pitch dark. They got undressed. Albert could feel the creature's gaze burning into him from the corner of the room, and who knows, maybe it could see in the dark. He had a strategy to deal with that eventuality too. When they were both naked, he drew his king-size duvet over them.

It was hot and sweaty inside their cocoon, but at last, at long last he got an erection and kept it up. His worst fear had been that the creature wouldn't accept his disappearing from view, and would find its way into the limited space, but that didn't happen.

It was still out there, but the wine had dulled his perceptions, and he was able to ignore its presence. When he finally thrust into Olivia everything else was swept away in a wave of warm, wet bliss. It was even better than he could possibly have imagined.

After a couple of minutes he just couldn't hold back, and it was as if every nerve in his body contracted into a tight, taut bundle before exploding outwards and downwards in a network of sparkling threads. As he rolled off Olivia and threw back the duvet, he knew that he had experienced something he never wanted to be without.

He switched on the bedside lamp and they lay there naked, caressing each other's sweaty skin. Albert felt a sense of calm that was almost as wonderful as the act of love itself, but in a tranquil way. Something had been emptied out of him, and peace had seeped in in its place. His normal defense mechanisms were down, and before he could stop himself the words slipped out: "Olivia, do you get the feeling that something's... watching us?"

Instinctively Olivia covered her breasts with the duvet and looked around the room. "What do you mean?"

"No, it's just, I mean, wow, that was fantastic."

The heat in Albert's face increased noticeably. It was many years since he had come out with such an atrocious sentence. Olivia smiled and said "Mmm," then got out of bed to go to the bathroom. Albert stayed where he was and watched her go. His thoughts were flowing freely, and as if it had never been a problem he formed the command in his head and transmitted it towards the corner: Go away. Leave me.

Nothing happened. The creature carried on looking at him. Now he had formulated the thought, Albert realized this was what he wanted. He no longer needed the creature's guarantee, he wanted to be free to live his life without its constant surveillance, he wanted to be able to do that wonderful thing with Olivia without resorting to special measures. He could hear the shower running in the bathroom, and he propped himself up on one elbow and said the words out loud: "Go away. Leave me."

He could feel the nature of the creature's attention shift; he knew it had heard and understood what he said. But it didn't leave him, it didn't move a fraction of an inch from its place. Albert slumped back on the pillow and covered his eyes with his arm.

This can't go on. I have to put an end to it.

By the time Olivia emerged from the bathroom, Albert was up and dressed.

"What are you doing?" she said, holding a towel in front of her as if she was suddenly conscious of her nakedness.

"I'm sorry," Albert said, "but I forgot—there's something I have to do."

"Now? It's after ten!"

"I know. But I have no choice."

"So... Do you want me to leave, or what?"

"You can stay if you like. I'll be back."

"Oh yes, I can have a nice chat with your mom and dad, tell them what it was like having sex for the first time."

"Listen, I'm really sorry…"

"So am I."

With tears in her eyes, Olivia gathered up her clothes and got dressed. Albert sat on the bed watching her, not saying a word. The creature sat in the corner, watching him. As Olivia was on her way out through the door, Albert said: "Olivia? I love you."

She glanced over her shoulder and said: "Prove it, then". Albert could hear her crying as she opened the front door and closed it behind her. He glowered at the corner of his room and whispered: "Go away! Go away!"

Nothing happened.

Oswald was surprised when Albert called him. He said it wasn't really convenient, and Albert had to entice him with the promise of both future Cthulhu sessions and friendship—neither of which he intended to provide—before Oswald gave in and said he could come 'round.

Oswald was one of the few members of the class who didn't live in a house. It felt kind of exotic as Albert took the subway to Blackeberg, then used the GPS on his phone to find his way to Elias Lönnrots väg. The slums, you could say. The shabby three-storey apartment blocks, the broken street lamps, the uneven sidewalks, the gaping potholes.

Oswald lived right down at the end, in the innermost section off a gloomy courtyard with not a tree or a shrub in sight, just carelessly parked cars and chained-up bicycles with no air in the tires. The sound of Albert's footsteps bounced off the dark facades as he made his way over to the outside door of Oswald's block and yanked it open.

The hallway reeked of fried food and cheap detergent, and by the time Albert rang Oswald's doorbell he felt as if he was coming down with something. The ugliness of the place was like an infection, and the situation didn't improve when Oswald opened the door. A musty, yeasty smell mingled with smoke seeped out into the already noxious stairwell, and Albert had to stop himself from covering his nose with his hand.

"Hi," he said.

"Hi," Oswald replied, making no move to let him in. Oswald was wearing a faded black T-shirt with the words Miskatonic University School of Literature on it. He looked pale and unwell.

"Can I come in?"

"What for?"

"Like I said... I really need to talk to you. It's very, very important, and you're the only one who can help me."

Oswald sighed and his shoulders drooped. "Don't bother taking off your shoes," he said. "Just come in."

Once Albert was in the hallway, Oswald steered him towards an open door, but Albert still had time to notice the state the apartment was in. The wallpaper was peeling, and there were heaps of old newspapers everywhere, stuff all over the place. As Albert passed the kitchen he saw piles of dirty dishes.

Before he went into Oswald's room he glanced into the living room. It was in darkness, but the light from the hallway enabled him to see a table covered with bottles and overflowing ashtrays, and a woman slumped on the sofa, her long, dirty hair trailing onto the floor.

What a fucking dump.

Albert had never experienced anything like this. Oswald's apartment was like a dirty parody of a haunted house, so disgusting that it didn't feel real. Fortunately Oswald's room was a slight improvement, even though Albert's nose told him it hadn't been cleaned for quite some time. Two large bookcases dominated the space, which was otherwise occupied only by a desk with an ancient desktop computer, and a bed which surprisingly enough had been made. Albert went over to the shelves and ran his finger over the spines of the books.

He recognized several names: Lovecraft, Robert Bloch, Ramsey Campbell, Robert E Howard. Others were unfamiliar to him, and some books didn't have any writing on the spine, or else the spine had fallen off.

"Sit down," Oswald said, pointing to his bed. Albert was about to make an acidic comment in response, but thought better of it. He obediently sat down on the bed, which was lumpy and uncomfortable. Oswald took the desk chair, resting his chin on his interlinked fingers. "So?"

Albert took a deep breath, then told him the whole story. The evening they had played the game, the spell he had intoned, the arrival of the creature he suspected of being a star vampire. The way it had followed him wherever he went. He left out the events that had taken place earlier that evening; obviously he would have liked to boast about the fact that he'd had sex with Olivia, but he didn't want to make Oswald jealous. When he'd finished, he asked: "Do you believe me?"

Oswald nodded slowly. "Yes. Is it here now?"

Albert pointed towards the bookcases. The creature reached almost all the way up to the ceiling; it billowed out into the room, stretching towards Oswald. "There."

Oswald glanced sideways, then turned his attention back to Albert. "And what was it you wanted to talk about?"

Albert snorted and shook his head. If Oswald believed his story, then his calm demeanor was incomprehensible. The creature's malevolent presence was on the point of swallowing him up, and yet he was just sitting there. Several disparaging remarks occurred to Albert, but then he thought of Olivia. Of that soft, moist wonderful experience that could be his once more if only he found a way, so instead he said: "I want to know if there's a spell to get rid of it."

Oswald stared at him. For a long time. His gaze travelled up from Albert's loafers to his Acne jeans and his Fred Perry sweatshirt, and finally he looked Albert directly in the eye.

"And if there is," he said, "why should I tell you?"

Albert's parents were home by the time he got back. His father had gone up to bed, while his mother was sitting at the kitchen table with her usual camomile tea. Albert poured himself half a cup, sat down opposite her and asked if the play had been good.

"Yes... Not particularly uplifting, but it was very intense and the acting was excellent. I thought Olivia would still be here—has something happened?"

"No, she just had to go home, that's all."

"I saw the prawn shells in the trash..."

"Mmm."

Silence. Albert sipped his tea. His mother leaned forward, looking concerned. "Are you okay, sweetheart? Is something bothering you?"

Albert kept his eyes fixed on the table. Something was bothering him. Perhaps his defenses had been breached after the evening's rollercoaster of ecstasy and despair; the words just came out.

"What if I'm... evil?"

His mother frowned. "Why on earth would you be evil, sweetheart? Where's this come from—is it something to do with that game of yours?"

"No, it's nothing." Albert got to his feet. "Night Mom."

Albert went into his room, locked the door, connected his phone to his computer and downloaded the pictures he had taken in Oswald's apartment. He had simply waved his cell phone around and clicked a few times on his way to the front door; Oswald hadn't noticed a thing.

After running the images through a photo editing program and improving the exposure and definition, the wretchedness of Oswald's home was crystal clear. Albert had even managed to snap the woman who was presumably Oswald's mother, and if he wasn't mistaken, that patch by the sofa was vomit. He adjusted the contrast to make it stand out even more.

Oswald had refused to tell him anything, but had hinted that De Vermis Mysteriis wasn't an invention at all, but was in fact a real book, and that he might just have a copy. He wouldn't say another word.

It was obvious that Oswald was ashamed of the conditions in which he lived, and Albert had decided to pressurize him on this sensitive issue in order to make him reveal what he knew. He downloaded the improved images onto his phone and went through them just to check that they were sufficiently humiliating even on the smaller screen. Perfect.

He went to bed, curling up under the duvet that still smelled of what he and Olivia had done, and thought about his final option. If Oswald continued to refuse in spite of everything, then Albert could set the creature onto him. It seemed reasonable to choose Oswald, since he was the only one who understood what it was all about. If Oswald didn't cooperate, then he would have to take the consequences.

The more Albert thought about it, the less malicious it seemed to him. Oswald had only himself to blame if he didn't take into account the resources at his opponent's disposal. All's fair in love and war, et cetera et cetera.

Albert had grown so used to the creature's presence in his room that he had consigned the sound it made to a corner of his consciousness where it no longer bothered him. Tonight, however, when he had turned out the light, that demented giggling was unusually clear. As if it really could read his mind, and was looking forward to what tomorrow might bring.

3

THE OPPORTUNITY AROSE during the lunch hour. It was a fine autumn day, the air high and clear, and a lot of the students were outside. Even Oswald, who usually spent recess lurking in the library, was leaning against the post to which the basketball goal was fixed. Albert went over to him.

"So," he said. "Have you given any more thought to what we talked about yesterday?"

Oswald kicked at a broken hockey stick and shook his head. "Nope. Why should I?"

"So you're not going to tell me what to do?"

Oswald glanced at Albert. There were dark shadows under his eyes, and when he smiled Albert could see a yellow film covering his teeth, as if he hadn't cleaned them for quite some time.

"You don't get it," he said. "You really don't get it."

"Possibly not," Albert replied, taking out his phone. He clicked on the folder of photographs from Oswald's apartment and showed him a couple of them. "But I do get the fact that you wouldn't want me to share these. On Facebook, for example."

Up until that moment everything had gone according to Albert's script. Right now Oswald was supposed to look around in horror, beg Albert to put away his phone, then agree to help him. But that wasn't what happened at all.

Albert began to sense that there might be a problem when Oswald gazed at the pictures with a total lack of interest rather than blind panic, but the real deviation from Albert's plan occurred when Oswald picked up the hockey stick and slammed it against the basketball post, the sound reverberating around the schoolyard like a church bell.

People turned to see what was going on; Oswald raised his arms, waving like a drowning man, and yelled at the top of his voice; "Hey everyone—come over here! Albert's got something to show you!"

The students had nothing in particular to do, and were drawn to whatever was going on like wasps to a pot of honey—something sweet to alleviate the boredom.

"What the fuck are you doing?" Albert hissed.

Oswald showed those yellow teeth again. "You're laboring under a misapprehension, Albert, if you think I have something to lose."

A circle of interested observers had gathered around them, and Albert realized he was screwed, for the moment at least. He was sufficiently socially aware to know that he couldn't possibly pass his phone around. Posting pictures on Facebook and adding "Check this out!" in passing was one thing; demonstrating physical responsibility for the action was something else altogether. It would appear mean-spirited, vengeful and downright nasty. Demeaning.

Fortunately getting out of the situation was no problem; all he had to do was dismiss Oswald's trumpeting as yet another sign of his stupidity. Albert had nothing to show them. There were a lot of people now, including Olivia. Albert tried to catch her eye but she was looking only at Oswald, who had stopped waving his arms. He pointed at Albert and said: "This is Albert—you all know him. Albie. He came 'round to see me last night to ask for my help with something, and when he didn't get it he took some pictures that he'd like to show you."

Okay, so that was his game. Clever. One point to Oswald. He had made it impossible for Albert to post the photos online; Albert couldn't stand here denying that he had any pictures, then share them later on.

For a moment Albert didn't know what to do. He hadn't considered this possibility. Or rather impossibility. Oswald's behavior was so out of character that there was no way Albert could have predicted it, and in the heat of the moment the best he could come up with was: "I've no idea what you're talking about, Oswald. Chill out."

Oswald did not chill out. The stage belonged to him. In a voice full of a hitherto unsuspected power, he yelled: "My name is Oswald, but most of you probably know me as the Whoopee Cushion. By the way, it was Albert here who came up with that name, along with a whole load of other stuff that you might not remember. But I do."

The Whoopee Cushion? When was that? Back in seventh grade? It was ages since anyone had called Oswald that, or at least since the beginning of ninth grade. As far as Albert could recall. He stared balefully at Oswald, who had worked himself up so much that a little bit of white foam was visible at the corners of his mouth. Albert rolled his eyes to show that this was nothing to do with him; he was about to walk away when Oswald went on: "Yes, Albie's very inventive, but not so inventive that he can come up with a way of getting it up, in spite of the fact that he's with one of the prettiest girls in school."

Albert glanced at Olivia, who had gone bright red, and the fury of embarrassment surged through his body like poison.

"Be careful!" he hissed at Oswald. "Be very, very careful!"

Apparently ignoring the danger which he must know was threatening him, Oswald continued: "Albie thinks he's better than everyone else, but if he sees a naked girl his tiny little prick shrivels up like a frightened slug." A few people laughed, which encouraged Oswald to expand still further. "I mean what do I know, it could be something to do with his mother. She always used to..."

With those words, he crossed the line. Albert didn't care whether Oswald was crazy or suicidal or whether he really believed he had nothing to lose. He had crossed the line.

Kill him.

Albert formulated the words like a scream inside his head, like letters of fire. The creature loomed up in front of the children's climbing frame, and in the harsh light Albert could see it shimmering with a clarity he had never experienced before.

Kill him. Suck him dry!

Nothing happened, and Albert was so overwhelmed with boiling rage that he shouted the words out loud, in the direction of the climbing frame: "Kill him! Kill Oswald! Now!"

Silence descended on the assembled students and Albert understood why, realized what he sounded like, but he didn't care. As long as it happened. But it didn't happen. Albert's social radar picked up on the fact that people were edging away, because many of them thought that his murderous exhortation was directed at them. Through the silence came Oswald's voice, and this time he was addressing Albert directly.

"It wasn't you, Albert. How stupid can a person be?"

Albert looked at Oswald, whose smile was now so broad that the yellow teeth formed the rictus grin of a predator. A horrible suspicion suddenly struck him. "What are you talking about?"

Deliberately assuming a deep voice, Oswald intoned: "Ph'nglui mglw'nafh Cthulhu R'lyeh... did you really believe all that? A load of made-up crap from the rule book? There are genuine texts, Albert, texts you've never seen. But I have."

The suspicion became a certainty. "It was you who..."

"Yes. It was me."

The evening when they had played the game. Albert, repeating his made-up incantation with such feeling that he had begun to believe in it himself. Oswald's lips, moving in what Albert had thought was terror evoked by the power of suggestion, but in fact Oswald had been reciting the real spell. The tears in Oswald's eyes had been tears of joy at having succeeded, perhaps for the first time.

He is the flame. I am the candle. Which will be consumed.

Albert had to lean on the basketball post for support as everything he had thought he knew was turned upside down. The bell rang, and the crowd began to disperse.

"I don't understand," he whispered. "You haven't... you haven't given it a command."

"Oh yes I have," Oswald replied. "I told it to watch you. And to kill you when I say so. Or if I should die."

Albert's knees gave way and he sank to the ground as he protested feebly: "But. That's. Two. Things."

Above his head he heard Oswald laughing. "You mean it should be following the rule book? Pull yourself together, Albert. Grow up." Oswald patted him on the head. "If I allow you to do so."

Oswald's feet disappeared from Albert's peripheral vision as he headed for the school building. Behind him Albert could feel the creature's gaze licking his back. Weighing him up. Waiting.

He had thought he was in possession of an ever-present weapon that was his to fire. The weapon was there, it would always be there, but it was Oswald's finger that was resting on the trigger. From now on Albert would have to live with the knowledge that he could die at any moment. Just like that. Like pressing a button.

When Albert finally managed to raise his head, he felt as if a sandbag weighing several tons had been placed on the back of his neck. All the students had gone to class, except for one person. Felix. His arms were folded across his broad chest. He nodded pensively, unfolded his arms and began to walk towards Albert.

CELEBRATING TWENTY YEARS OF LILJA'S LIBRARY: AN AFTERWORD

I HOPE YOU enjoyed the stories in this book as much as I do. Each and every one of them are special in their own way. And now, before I leave you I want to thank a few people who were essential to this book that you hold in your hands. If not for them, this book and the site might not have happened at all. So please join me as I give them the recognition they so well deserve:

Stephen King: Thanks for letting me include your story "The Blue Air Compressor" and for giving me something to write about for the last 20 years. And for all the stories!

Jack Ketchum: Thanks for suggesting the "The Net" for this anthology. I'm so happy to have it included.

P.D. Cacek: Thanks for agreeing when Jack suggested "The Net" for the anthology.

Stewart O'Nan: Thanks for joining me in this anthology with your story. It's an important one!

Bev Vincent: Thanks for letting me be the first to publish your story about the wonderful Aeliana and also for being there with all the answers to whatever questions I have thrown at you for the last 20 years.

Clive Barker: Thanks for letting me publish "Pidgin and Theresa." It's one of the strangest and best stories I have ever read.

Brian Keene: Thanks for the story "An End to All Things." It's depressing and I totally love it!

Richard Chizmar: Thanks for letting me include your story and for publishing my books.

Kevin Quigley: Thanks for your story, friendship, and support during all these years!

Ramsey Campbell: Thanks for "The Companion." A great story about one of my favorite subjects.

Edgar Allan Poe: I hope you look down at us from where you are. Thanks for every author you have influenced!

Brian James Freeman: Thanks for offering "A Mother's Love" and for helping me through all the hurdles with doing a book like this. I couldn't have done it without you!

John Ajvide Lindqvist: Thanks for writing "The Keeper's Companion" for my anthology and thanks for involving me with the translation.

Marsha DeFilippo: Thanks for all your help during the last 20 years.

Anders Jakobson: Thanks for all your help with the website. Whatever I have wanted you have delivered. The site wouldn't be what it is today without you! It might not be at all.

Glenn Chadbourne: Thanks for creating Marv.

Marlaine Delargy: Thanks for a great translation of John's "The Keeper's Companion."

Mark Miller: Thanks for helping me get the rights to use "Pidgin and Theresa."